The gown fell. Her breasts shone snowy white in the starlight. I went to her; carried her to a couch nearby. My hands felt her skin turning from chill to warm to fiery—

With this highborn woman, love was different from what it had ever been before. There was no thought of proficiency, or of good or bad, right or wrong. Because of her, it was right; it was meant to be; it was *destined*.

*Even our bodies offered us proof. It seemed as if we fit each other perfectly. As if the gods had designed and crafted us to please no partners but each other. We shared a joyous moment—no, many long and increasingly ardent moments—and then we shared a final ecstasy I suspect only the gods and a few rare mortals are ever allowed to know. . . .*

Other Pinnacle Books by John Jakes:

I, BARBARIAN
VEILS OF SALOME
KING'S CRUSADER

# John Jakes

## THE MAN FROM CANNAE

(a new, revised, and enlarged edition
of the original work previously written
under the pseudonym of Jay Scotland)

PINNACLE BOOKS      LOS ANGELES

THE MAN FROM CANNAE

A Pinnacle Books edition of an original novel,
*The Traitor's Legion,* previously published by Ace Books
in 1963 under the pseudonym Jay Scotland. Published
by special arrangement with Lyle Kenyon Engel.
Produced by Lyle Kenyon Engel, Canaan, New York

ISBN: 0-52340-161-2

First printing, November 1977

Cover illustration by Len Goldberg

*Printed in the United States of America*

PINNACLE BOOKS, INC.
One Century Plaza
2029 Century Park East
Los Angeles, California 90067

*This time, for Nina.*

# Contents

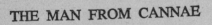

# THE MAN FROM CANNAE

# SPECIAL INTRODUCTION TO THE
# PINNACLE EDITION

Chronologically, this is the last of six historical novels "Jay Scotland" wrote years ago. It's also the only one written, so to speak, through the wrong end of a telescope.

One publisher brought out the first two Scotlands (*I, Barbarian*, and *Veils of Salome*), then lost interest. Another house published the final four; this is the fourth of that quartet, conceived and put on paper in 1962.

Then as now, publishing was to some extent a business of trend-following. This was demonstrated to me when the editor and I exchanged letters in which we struggled to come up with a subject I liked, but one which he thought was commercially feasible.

I'd already produced one novel dealing with ancient Rome, and I had a notion about writing a book on the American Revolution, or perhaps the French and Indian War. But I was told that—to paraphrase it—"guys in three-cornered hats don't make it."

The editor wanted another story about Rome. He said Rome was sure-fire. People automatically anticipated an exciting tale when they spied chariots, lolling emperors, and gladiatorial togs on a florid cover. So Rome it was.

At the time all this pulling and hauling took place, a minor boomlet in historical fiction was coming to an end for most publishers and most authors except permanently established ones such as Frank Slaughter and Frank Yerby. *The Man from Cannae* turned out to be my last effort before the boom went bust. Shortly after the publication of this piece, virtually no one in the nation would pick up a historical novel any longer.

That is, publishers said virtually no one in the nation would pick up a historical novel any longer. Sometimes I suspect the public was never consulted. But perhaps that's wrong. Perhaps, for some still-unexplained reason, readers did shy away from historicals for a while.

But to go back to '62—once there was agreement that I'd do another Roman book, choices of material and treatment were left to me. After some days of library-sitting and eyestrain, I ran across a reference to Hannibal, the famous Carthaginian general. Ah!

Yes, thought the editor, an interesting possibility. Then he got to musing via special delivery letters. The story of Hannibal Barca was pretty well known, at least in broad outline. What about handling it from the other end? With the Carthaginian as the menace? The enemy? I wistfully abandoned plans to cross the Alps on yellow copy paper and began reading further. When I unearthed an account of the battle of Cannae (pronounced kań—ē) and its aftermath, I knew the editor had hit on a good idea.

The timetable of the story runs from 216 B.C., the year of Cannae, to 211 B.C., in the long campaign historians term the Second Punic War. (Regardless of their ancestry, all Carthaginians were lumped together as "Punic" people; the adjective derives from another word meaning Phoenician.) In constructing the book, I did take a few liberties with the time span, compressing events here and there. But most of the incidents follow the record.

After Cannae, for example, the outraged and terrified Roman populace did turn on Varro's ten thousand and send them packing to Sicily in disgrace.

Also, the war engines of Archimedes did exist as described—granting our trust in authorities such as Plutarch.

Hannibal's secret journey was invented. But such a trip is certainly not beyond possibility. Syracuse was of great interest to Hannibal because of its critical role in control of the sea routes to Africa. And we do know the general often made personal inspections of critical areas—without military trappings, and incognito. When I discovered the historical record is murky concerning Hannibal's exact whereabouts at certain periods during the years 212-210, I decided I could send him to Syracuse.

After *The Man from Cannae* was completed and published, I looked back on it with considerable fondness. First, I thought the notion of writing about Hannibal from the point of view of his opponents had worked into a fairly exciting story. Second, as previously noted, it was the last historical novel I was able to sell. I soon had a file drawer of ideas and rejected outlines. I still have them.

Some mile-markers on a trip are remembered vividly after most others are forgotten. This is one of the remembered ones, because it symbolizes a long interruption of a journey not resumed for a decade—

When, at last, I was able to trot out those "guys in three-cornered hats" in the first of the Kent family novels.

JOHN JAKES

# Part One

# HANNIBAL'S HEROES

# CHAPTER I

# BATTLEFIELD

The shaft that came striking for my guts was not held in the hand of one of the howling Numidian horsemen who rode for the general they called the Thunderbolt. The shaft was held in the hand of one of my own kind.

In the great swirling clouds of dust blown by the scorching summer wind, men turned to ghosts on the battlefield. A rider suddenly appeared in that whirling, blowing confusion, galloping fast through a break between bands of mounted Romans and Carthaginians locked in death struggle. Time ran out for me then, as it had run out for our army, cleverly trapped on this plain of Cannae by Hannibal's forty thousand.

The rider thundered down, the sharp tip of his iron pilum flashing once in brittle sunlight. He held the Roman spear tight against his side as he rode, his hand as white as his crazed, smiling face. Then, above screams

3

of men and animals, the clang of blades against blades, the vain bleats of our trumpets and bugles, a new flurry of hoofbeats hammered behind me.

Sword in my right fist, I used my other hand to swing my mount's head half around. And that way I saw three enemies in place of just one; the pair charging from behind me were grinning Numidian devils riding without reins. Their white robes flew in the dusty wind. From the other direction, his crippled leg slung out stiffly in special stirrup gear, rode the one I needed to fear most—

This was Sardus Pulvius the nobleman. The member of Rome's knightly order of *equites*. The master of horse under our commander, the consul Terentius Varro.

By rights, Sardus Pulvius should have given thought to rallying our cavalry units crumbling under the pounding attack of Hannibal's African horse. Instead he only wanted the blood of a fellow Roman soldier— mine.

I kicked the belly of my horse. The weary beast lunged forward as Pulvius thundered at me. His thrust went wide and he plunged by. One of the Numidians whipped up his sword and screeched like a fiend. Pulvius's pilum, driven by the force of his charge, plunged straight through the man's throat.

There was a fountain of blood, enough to strike my cheeks as I jerked my mount around. The warm, stinking stuff ran down my face into my armor. The second Numidian galloped his pony past his dead comrade who was still erect in the saddle. Pulvius tried to wrench the pilum out of the corpse. All around me I could hear the cries of the maimed, the oaths of those

4

still fighting, the rattle of swords. Somehow Varro had bungled. We had been lured into a trap, and beaten.

But that would make no difference if either the Numidian or Pulvius killed me.

With another of those damnable yells that demoralized the legions the first time we heard them, the remaining Numidian bore down on me. I guided my horse backwards frantically, raising my sword to parry at the same time.

"Don't let him kill you, Prefect!" came a shout. "I mean to be the one."

The Numidian's mount collided with mine, reared and screamed and rolled its eyes, then reared again. The laugh of the man who had yelled disappeared under the noise of two horses kicking at each other. The Numidian reached across to try to throttle me. I drove my right arm out and upward, hard.

Sun flashed off the flat of the blade, a dazzle of light. Then iron hit something soft, next something harder, and grated. I had gone through flesh and then I had gone through bone.

Under my legs my mount jumped, in convulsions. I flung myself away and sprawled in the dust. I staggered to my feet and wiped the sweat out of my eyes. Wearily I turned my head from side to side. Men thundered by, riding very hard, looking near to suffocating in their armor. Sixty thousand legionnaires had gone against Hannibal's forty thousand. But we were being destroyed by the bungling idiot who led us, as much as by our enemies. Perhaps more than by our enemies.

I needed a horse. Mine had fallen with a javelin through its bowels. My *ala*—the squadron of cavalry that I commanded as *praefectus equitum*—had ceased to exist in a flash of swords. And still I could not find Pulvius in all of the dust and racket.

But he found me.

Hoofs hammered in the dust at my back. I turned wildly, striking for his horse's neck. My sword glanced against the shaft of his pilum as he thrust down. With a snap, my blade broke in half, the pilum having caught it at the hilt. Then he was by and wheeling.

I saw a Numidian sword lying up a little hillside and darted for it.

"Yes, run!" Pulvius's horse was in motion again as he shouted. "Make the sport all the better, Prefect!"

Above the slight slope another contingent of Roman cavalry galloped in frantic retreat. I didn't like the lighter feel of the African weapon. But it was all I had. Pulvius was coming up the hillside, his leather-wrapped left leg stiff as a pillar of wood in the long stirrups.

Up swept his right arm, drawing back the pilum. Perhaps he expected me to stand and to try to dodge him. Instead, I threw myself forward. I doubled over, toward his horse. With a long sweep of my hand I hacked the cutting edge of the Numidian blade down the barrel of his animal. The wound wasn't deep, but blood gushed and it surely hurt. The animal reared. Pulvius gave an astonished cry and tumbled to earth.

Right then I should have opened his throat and let the blood flow. And yet, I did not—

Perhaps I didn't fully grasp the reality of all that was happening. I knew well that he hated me, yet I couldn't believe that such hatred could exert itself when the very fate of Rome was in the balance, and her men should have been fighting together.

A man going to war normally supposes he can count on those men who fight on his side; who wear the same

6

uniform that he does. Of course, there will be conflict between engagements on the battlefield, small disputes or even large ones. But it is expected that when the official enemy arrives, then the men in similar uniforms will forget their differences and group together, will go to help each other in case of need—even die for each other.

All that is part of the sad singularity of war. War unites, it would seem, as peace never can. The call to arms is heard, and it gives men a chance to fight for something vastly more important than their daily bread; to be part of a cause; to submerge themselves in a whole greater than the individual warrior can ever be. That is the way it has always been—

Yet here before me was something almost unbelievably different:

A man of Rome, as I was a man of Rome, hating me with all his heart and soul—if he could be said to have either. A man hating me more than he hated the enemy. A man who recognized no uniform; a man of death and not just of war—

Pulvius was gasping as he clambered to his feet. For several moments we had been alone at the bottom of the little gully. Bands of horsemen continued to stream by above. Pulvius watched me, chuckling through parched, unsmiling lips. And then I understood why none of Hannibal's riders troubled to gallop down and kill us. Bigger game was running ahead of them—

The whole of the Roman Empire was running ahead of them.

A band of fierce Balearian slingers ran by at the top of the slope. Some of them were dancing and cavorting. One waved aloft the gilt *aquila* of a legion. I felt sickened. When our men no longer had the sacred gold

7

eagle standard in their possession, then truly the day was lost.

Pulvius slowly hitched himself toward me. He had difficulty walking due to his crippled left leg, which no longer bent at all. The fault was mine. That was what put the reckless shine into his black eyes, and ruined his handsome patrician face. He was about ten years older than I, perhaps in his thirty-fifth or sixth year. Taller and more powerful, too. The leg I had caused to be crippled left a trail as he dragged it along. His pilum glowed in the sunlight.

"Remember, Master Linus Julius?" he said to me. "Remember how I got this?" He whacked the greave on his left thigh, again and again.

"It was you who wanted the horse race," I said. "You who thought yourself the better rider."

"To this day I am the better rider. And I mean to leave your gutless body as proof."

I waved toward the horsemen thundering by. "With the army routed, how can you think about—?"

"The gods will deal with the Carthaginians," he broke in, hitching forward again. "I will deal with you and I will do it now."

# CHAPTER II

# DUEL

I knew he would not be persuaded otherwise. The hate reached back too far—

One night long months ago, I, a man of lower rank—an upstart cavalryman with too much wine in him—had wagered I could win a horse race against him, even though he was an *equite,* a noble of the knightly rank, whose training since birth had taught him everything about horsemanship. And he had never forgotten or forgiven me the incident which had occurred when we raced.

On a final turn our horses crashed together by chance. It was Pulvius who fell. His left leg was never straight again. Over the hoofbeats on the battlefield, the moans of men in their death-throes, the sounds of panic and retreat, I seemed to hear screaming from a surgeon's tent where they had vainly tried to straighten his leg.

9

There had been a crippling in his mind, too. Only I hadn't known that until now. Not until the battle had given him the chance to kill me undiscovered.

He smiled, very close now, making little jabs at my throat with the pilum, withdrawing it and jabbing yet again:

"Raise up your sword, Master Linus Julius. Raise up that little African sword. See whether it can stand against this piece of good Roman iron."

"I will not fight you," I said. "I fight the Carthaginians, not my own officers."

"Yet you didn't mind bragging to your own officers about your skill in the saddle, did you?" He swiped at sweat and dust on his face. "You didn't mind challenging the highest-ranking cavalry officer in the army, did you? That's because you're a low man, Linus Julius. Scum! You're only in the legion because your lot was drawn, not because your station makes it an honor to serve—"

"In the name of the gods!" I shouted. "We are both *on the same side!* We must escape—"

"Escape, hell! You did this to my leg, you vile, bragging clod! How long do you think I've waited for this moment?"

And even as the last words spewed from his mouth, he hurled himself forward, both hands on the haft of his pilum. In his wild black eyes shone the agony of knowing his grace and handsomeness had been destroyed forever.

I thrust the Numidian blade forward in an arc to parry the pilum. He cursed when the sword held the spear from descending any further. Then he kicked my leg. It was a gutter trick, unbefitting a nobleman, but

10

the pain was real and sharp. My leg slid out from under me in the dust. I went to one knee.

Sardus Pulvius tightened both hands around the pilum haft and brought the weapon toward my bare throat. I rolled over to my side and chopped with the Numidian blade. He cried out. Simultaneously my blade sliced a long strip of flesh off the inner side of his right arm as he leaned down. The pain made him jerk on the pilum.

Lying on my side in the dust, I was a relatively slim target. Nothing else saved me. The pilum's tip sliced under the hinges of my armor, through my tunic into the flesh of my right shoulder blade. I bit down until blood ran over my lips. Then the pilum pulled free.

I had no strength to do more than hack feebly at his ruined left leg. The blade ran harmlessly against bronze. He kicked again. His heavy boot smashed under my jaw. My head snapped back to the ground. The sun behind the dust clouds swelled into a giant ball and turned deep red.

"Let me kick your brains out instead, Prefect—"

His shadow fell upon me. All across my back the light but deep wound spread warm blood. Sardus Pulvius, the descendant of the Pulvian Gens, hauled back his crippled leg and kicked once more. This time he hit the side of the jaw.

A hundred places in my head seemed to hurt all at once. "Watch your brains come out like the upstart dog you are!" Pulvius was panting, nearly incoherent. The boot slammed against my head another time.

Feebly I grabbed for that boot. He dragged himself back, his form obscuring the sun. The pilum glittered as he took a new grip. I lay prone, too weak to resist further—

11

*"The road junction! The road junction in Venusia! Meet there! Pulvius, follow us!"*

Who was shouting? There had been a brief lull as the battle tide swept on. But now the sound of hoofs was loud again. All at once stones began to rattle down around us. Pulvius cursed. The voice that had shrilled a moment ago came again, closer this time:

"Pulvius! We have a mount for you! Up and follow me! The Balearians with their slings are on us."

"General," Pulvius shouted back, "here is a man I must—"

"Pulvius, the horse, in Mars's name! That's one of our own men! Let him die if he's hurt. Escape while you have the chance. You are an important officer!"

Pulvius's face grew dark, or so I thought. My own eyesight was dimming as the blood leaked out of the hole in my back. I saw the terrible whiteness of his knuckles around the pilum's haft. But he could not bring himself to strike: the voice that had shouted from the top of the rise belonged to Terentius Varro himself, the plebeian consul who had taken command today.

"Master Pulvius," someone else shouted, "General Varro orders you to ride with him. He will try to re-group the army at the road junction in Venusia."

Pulvius had no choice. Rocks were falling everywhere, hard and deadly. Still another company of Hannibal's slingers was approaching. The officer helped Pulvius drag himself into the saddle. Pulvius followed the man up the slopes. At least he had been unwilling to do murder under the eyes of his commander. It said a little something for him, anyway; for his training; for his noble birth—

I turned over on my belly. A Balearian stone struck me on the back of the skull. I heard Pulvius shout:

12

"I think I've done my work, Prefect. Let the Carthaginians finish the job."

And he vanished down the plain, riding hard at the heels of Varro's party.

Cries of "Meet at the road junction at Venusia!" seemed to sound everywhere for a while. Soon they died out, and the Balearian slingstones ceased to fall. A company of heavy Carthaginian horse thundered by. After they had passed, I rose to hands and knees and crawled to the lip of the hill.

Already Varro's fleeing band of a hundred or so had disintegrated into smaller groups as the Carthaginian heavy horse pursued. The sun had passed its zenith. The plain sloped downward toward the sea on my right, upward to the ruined town of Cannae on my left. In that direction, amid more boiling clouds of dust in a sort of V-shaped valley, the last two surviving legions were hemmed in by the rest of the enemy army—and were being slaughtered.

Well, I cared no longer. Pulvius had done his work. So, too, it seemed, had the enemy general, Hannibal Barca, that wild and desperate man whom we Romans thought to be some evil god, since he had miraculously marched across the snow-covered Alps, where none had crossed before. He had entered Latium two years earlier, with thousands of men and forty war elephants.

I had joined the Ninth Legion a year and a half ago, leaving my uncle's farm near the great city of Rome. I had risen by dint of hard work to command a cavalry *ala*—a squadron—attached to my legion. In midsummer just a year ago, I had ridden forth against the Carthaginians at Lake Trasumenus. There, for the first time in remembered history, the fighting lines of the Roman legions had not stood fast under an assault. It

13

was the Carthaginian soldiers who carried the day—those same men we derisively called Carthaginians because they were Phoenician sea sailors at one time. They had begun their war upon Rome because their sea trade was slowly slipping away, being replaced by the domination of Roman trading galleys.

At that time, however, none had truly feared Hannibal Barca, whom everyone said was a ruthless but brainless monster. The debacle at Lake Trasumenus changed that. Afterwards, in panic, the Senate elected a military dictator, the first in the history of the Republic. He was warty old Quintus Fabius Maximus. "The Delayer" was what we came to call him. He trailed along behind Hannibal for a year after Trasumenus, in and out of valleys and mountain chains, never once engaging him—

Of the many mysteries of war, there is at least one as old as war itself. It is that the generals, with less to lose than the men, delay engagements for which the men are panting.

It may be that the men are in the throes of deep boredom, and even death itself seems preferable to further marching and waiting, waiting and marching. It is always the same. I do not know why.

At home, a general may win the reputation of being a fighter, a man who will go through hell in front of his troops and will not be stopped. This one is hailed as the Cleaver, that one as the Hatchet, the other one as the Thunderer. On the field, however—to the men under him—he is the yawner; the procrastinator; General Delay. It seems to be his duty to win with the fewest losses, and in pursuit of that duty, he risks the contempt of his soldiers.

Here is the oddest point of all: the men who live

through the eventual battle, who return to their wives and children, later call that particular general by the very same names the people at home always used. Having been cagey enough to see that some of his men survived, the general then becomes a hero in the eyes of those very survivors who once cursed him—

As it had turned out, there *was* a purpose to the Delayer's tactics. While he dawdled, eight fresh legions were being readied to meet the smaller army of Carthage—

Today at Cannae had been the bloody meeting. And now it was over. The day was lost—and I along with it.

Someone lifted me. From hhis speech, I knew it was a Carthaginian, but that was all I knew. My mind was growing dark. Pulvius had been right. What he had begun, they would finish.

Even if I managed to live a while longer, every Roman legionary knew Hannibal Barca killed his prisoners to provide sport for his men.

# CHAPTER III

# THE LORD FROM THE DARK

Fifty thousand Roman dead were the toll at Cannae that summer day. Fully eighty senators had perished. Also twenty-eight of forty-five military tribunes. And the man responsible, beyond any doubt, was Terentius Varro. Having followed the trail of the Carthaginian army for months without an engagement, he had finally decided to fight—

In a trap, as it turned out. Cannae was ground selected to favor Hannibal's cavalry, which operated at maximum efficiency on rough terrain. I learned it that same night, in a gruesome way:

Hands smacked briskly at my cheeks. I gagged and opened my eyes. Someone poured a sour wine into my mouth. I began to revive almost at once.

My shoulder hurt less, stinging with ointment and bound with a long piece of linen wrapped round and round my chest. Around me, voices spoke in a strange tone. Firelight flickered. Hands pushed me up to my feet. I rubbed my face and blinked—

Then their eyes told me.

They said the kindness they had shown was not kindness at all, and the bandage was only a way of making me ready for their enjoyment, which was to come soon.

The eyes shone black and fierce, a ring of them. They were Numidian eyes. The white-robed men squatted around a campfire by the silken command tents of their unit. On spears thrust into the dirt of the plain hung various pieces of my armor. They had left me a clout, but nothing else.

"We welcome you, Roman."

I turned, fully awake. The hands released me. The speaker swaggered up, a thin swarthy African whose deep mahogany skin contrasted with his dusty white robes. He touched my chin with the tip of his sword.

"Can you understand what I am saying to you?"

"Yes, I know the gutter Greek you Carthaginians speak."

"Your wound was deep. I trust that we have relieved the sting at least a bit."

"Do you expect my thanks for it? Kill me and get it done with!"

This caused him to smile. I thought that the smile was a sly one. All around him, the several dozen Numidians likewise looked amused as they sipped or guzzled from their wine bowls.

"Kill you? But you're an officer!" the leader said. "I bow to you, out of deep and abiding respect."

And he did. It became a gesture of contempt.

Then he tugged at his small black chin beard. "You

are young, Roman. On the thin side, too. But an officer, and alive. That combination is hard to come by this evening. Most all the officers are dead. My men wanted to take you to the pens they're putting up for the prisoners. I said no. We have had a long, hard fight. We deserve a little enjoyment, I think."

One of his hooked eyebrows raised, as if in inquiry. The desert cavalrymen crashed their bows on the ground, beating them in rhythm as a sign of approval. The wind against my naked flesh seemed unbearably cold.

The Numidian chief walked over to the embers of the fire. He kicked at them with a curl-toed boot.

"How is it you understand the Greek, officer?"

"My uncle raised me. He ran a horse farm before he died a year ago. He traded with many men from many countries. Thus I learned to talk with animals."

The Numidian had shown surprise at my willingness to answer. When I turned the words back on him, he stiffened with rage. He must have been one of the thousands whom Hannibal Barca had recruited in Africa, then brought to Spain and from there across the Alps into Italy. With a swoop, he pulled a brand out of the fire. Its end was bright cherry red.

"Mustapha! Zareem! Take his arms."

Two men sprang up to grab me. I lashed out with my elbows, then spat in their faces, then kicked and punched them. One of the men struck me in the small of the back. I fell. They dragged me up again, holding me tightly.

The officer passed the brand so near to my nose that I fancied I smelled the stink of my own flesh singeing. "Tonight, horse officer," he said, "when we took you for our prize—we recognized your armor and your in-

19

signia—we planned to amuse ourselves with you the whole evening. Now, however, I find that I don't like your nasty tongue and I dislike your overbearing ways even more. *We* won today, not you Romans. You seem to have forgotten."

Several of the men in the circle laughed. The Numidian played up to them, smiling:

"One day, horse officer, your Roman fathers will understand. The Lord Hannibal is as to your fat generals as the lion is to the chick. Or didn't you know—" He shoved the brand close to my jaw again. "Didn't you know it was a pretty trap we sprang? Is your ignorance the reason you strut so?"

Humiliation made my eyelids sting. "There was no trap! One bumbling, rash general, yes. But the rest—"

"Were led like plump little lambs." He left an arc of sparks as he gestured with the firebrand. "Weeks ago, Lord Hannibal chose this plain for the battle. Do you remember the outpost camp your soldiers ran across? With silver and gold spoils abandoned as though we feared the coming of the mighty Roman legions? Lord Hannibal, the clever fox, staged that. Those other incidents, too—parties of our horsemen fleeing away from your scouts, as though we were not strong enough to meet you. Drawing you on—drawing you on, all the time, you and your ignorant officers! That is a lesson you have yet to learn, Roman. We come from a strange land. So you think that we are witless barbarians—"

What he said was true; the generals had indeed believed that they fought savages. I confess I had believed the same thing.

Well, then, if Cannae was a trap, then perhaps we deserved what had happened to us—

Out in the torchlit darkness I heard a clank of chains. A procession of wounded legionnaries marched by slowly, Carthaginian guards at their sides. The Numidian officer signalled his men to close around and conceal me until the captives had passed.

Then the Numidians resumed their places in the circle. If we had mistaken their savage ways for lack of military skill, we had indeed been wrong. But savages they remained, I thought when I studied their eyes again.

"Let us not prolong this. My men are weary of waiting—"

So saying, the officer thrust the red-hot brand against the skin of my forehead.

Pain welled inside me, beating through my body. I tried to stiffen my legs, I tried to stand. I would not howl in fright. *I would not debase myself before these brutes—*

The officer laughed. "Come, come, pretty bird! Why so silent? Sing for us. Sing and cheep to us about your courage."

He touched the brand to my bare belly and held it.

*Held it—*

The rotten stench of burned skin rose up to gag me. I dropped to my knees, my head shaking from side to side. I tried to keep from crying out as they held on, refusing to let me fall. The officer shifted the brand to my back; touched it to the linen binding my wound. Had I known hell before, ever, I knew that this was worse— *"What am I leading? Warriors? Or a pack of beasts?"*

The thunderous shout had come from the darkness. The fire lifted away from my shoulder. I pitched forward as a great jabbering went up in the circle, then immediately was hushed away to silence.

Boots thudded in the dust. I heard curses in Greek.

"Lift him up before I give you a touch of fire yourself, Hasin!"

The Numidian's voice turned shaky: "My lord, we only meant to amuse ourselves by—"

"The prisoners belong in the prisoner pens. To be treated like men, not animals. Haven't I not told you this a hundred times and more?"

"A thousand and one times," Hasin muttered with unconsciously mocking solemnity.

"Watch your tongue or there'll be a new commander in these tents, Hasin."

"Thy word is law, Lord Hannibal!" came the sudden, anxious reply.

The name of our great enemy brought my eyes open in spite of the pain. The man, who had come striding out of the dark where a horse blew and stamped, was tall, black-eyed, and of good form. Apart from the rough, intelligent chiselling of his features, however, no one would have taken him for a man out of the ordinary. He wore no trappings of any kind. No enameled sword-sheath; no chains; no medals of office. Instead, what I could see of his uniform consisted of soft, plain leather boots and a long russet-colored coat of Spanish wool that reached nearly to the ground.

Under the hood of the cloak his black eyes glistened, and his small square beard also. His nose was sharp, giving him a slightly barbaric cast. And although he did not strike me as a mild man, neither did he resemble the butcher of whom all Rome spoke in whispers.

I swallowed, fought back the pain from the burns

and tried to see whether treachery lurked in that enigmatic gaze. He was an actor, of course; all great generals have that in them. Yet I detected no treachery as he said:

"Tell me your name and legion, soldier."

"Linus Julius. *Prefectus equitum* of the Ninth."

He spoke Greek smoothly and fluently: "And you are a Roman citizen?"

"All officers and all regular soldiers must be citizens."

"Yes, now I recall that. Well, officer, by the fortunes of war you are my prisoner. Killing on a battlefield is one thing. Killing a captive is entirely another. Hasin!"

The Numidian scurried forward. He was cowed now; cowed and gutless.

"Take him to the pens. If another spot of his hide is harmed, I will give you the fire against your belly as you tried to do with him."

Hannibal shook his head, then stared at me again:

"Times like these, I'm grateful that my father in the siege camp in Sicily taught me to keep a trunk of cloaks and wigs about. They never know—" He gestured to the warriors, almost like a sorrowing father himself. "—when their commander will come out of the dark like a common man. I will not bow down to Rome. But neither will I humble her at the price of turning loose an army of mad dogs."

"Why this generosity?" I asked. "Why not kill me now since you will do so eventually?"

"Then you believe the stories too?" It was impossible to read what was in his eyes; sadness, perhaps.

"Aren't they true?" I replied. "Hannibal, the red-handed butcher?"

His eyes sparked with anger, but it was quickly

23

supressed. "I will not spend time arguing with a prisoner over my methods of waging war. I will say only this. Do not judge me by the conduct of men like Hasin, but of what becomes of you in my pens."

Then a mocking little twinkle of mirth lighted the dark eyes. "Apart from purely humanitarian considerations, you are worth far more to me whole than you are in parts. Every living Roman soldier will be ransomed to his people. As a cavalryman, your price will be 500 denarii. I would caution you to thank your stars that I don't care over-much for slaughter."

He looked at me, but I kept silent.

"And you should also be thankful my war chest is growing empty. Think on these things and be grateful."

I nodded then; weary and hurt as I was, I knew he was right.

With a graceful gesture, surprising from him, he turned away from me. When he yelled, his voice was fierce:

"To the pens with him!"

# CHAPTER IV

# THE TRIBUNE

Guards opened the gates of the timber prisoner pens. With an outpouring of curses, the Numidians hurled me forward. I fell on my face and lay there, too stunned to move.

I felt or sensed a presence beside me. Someone was kneeling—

"Here, can you stand? There's a sponge full of wine left in the corner."

"I can stand," I croaked as he helped me up. "I can stand and go back and fight the whoresons who threw me in here like some lump of meat."

Quickly the man lifted a warning finger to his lips. He led me to a corner of the enclosure and drew the sponge out of a wood bucket.

"Time enough for action later," he cautioned.

"Boastful talk now will only cause the Carthaginians to tighten security. Whereas, if we seem meek and cooperative—"

He smiled in a cunning way. He was a tall, well-set-up man with graying hair and rather aristocratic features. I saw the shine of armor plate in the starlight.

I pointed. "That medal says you're a military tribune. I thought they were all dead."

"Most of us are, yes. My name is Octavius Terence."

He clapped my shoulder in a gesture of comradeship and drew me down beside the bucket. As I sucked wine from the sponge, my head slowly cleared. The tribune looked about with caution, then whispered, "Jupiter Stator knows why the lot has fallen to me to lead an escape attempt. There are few enough who want to go. Most prefer to remain and be ransomed."

I made a face. "A company of cowards. Has the great Hannibal frightened them to death?"

"From the looks of those burns, perhaps you have good reason to join the frightened."

I explained what had been done to me. "But although he saved me, Tribune, I don't believe Hannibal is so kind as to spare us solely for the sake of easing his conscience."

"Nor I," he said.

"Evidently he needs money—"

"—and prisoner ransom is a perfect way to refurbish his war chest, as he told you. No, I don't take that man for the fool he's played up to be by the windbags in the Senate. Reading him wrongly, we've been defeated. In truth, I have no stomach left for this war. But if Rome is near to falling after today, I suppose we are morally bound to do what we can."

"Odd talk for a tribune. More fitting for a philosopher."

Terence smiled wryly. He was perhaps ten years older than I, and spoke with a mildly cynical, world-weary manner.

"Yes, my father trained me in that and other gentlemanly pursuits. He prepared me as well for an exalted position in life. My father, you see, was a senator. But I have learned that philosophy has its place—which is not the field of war! We will not defeat the Carthaginians by reading books, no matter how valuable, nor by examining the entrails of the sacred chickens, as the old dictator Fabius seemed to like to do. Fighting is the only way. A dirty, inhuman business. But so is life itself." He shrugged. "No more lectures. We will try to get out tomorrow night. They will open the gates to feed us as they did this evening. How many will go, I cannot say."

"That makes no difference," I told him. "I will, whether I die or not."

He chuckled. "Still a fire-eater, are you? Well, that's all right. We can use every hand. I find that I don't even know who you are, now that I think of it."

Telling him, I realized that I liked this slightly embittered and obviously highly placed man. He was willing to risk his life for Rome, disgraced—and disgraceful—as she was. Knowing that much helped to temper my conviction that the noble class was weak, and indifferent to Hannibal's threat.

Then I remembered Pulvius a few hours ago, and realized that perhaps Octavius Terence was a rare exception—

I found a square patch of ground between the wounded who were lying or sitting forlorn in the dark.

Pain and weariness and a sense of defeat combined to lull me into a doze—

As night approached, I roused. Octavius Terence was moving among the men. Whispering; persuading.

Then I heard drunken voices from outside the wooden walls. Enemy guards were bragging that Hannibal would march directly on Rome from Cannae. Since the city was virtually defenseless and most of the army wiped out, Terence used this as an additional argument when he spoke to those around me.

As it was, many wanted to remain behind. No more than eighty of us were ready when the gates swung open the following nightfall.

"Here is the pig swill for the fine Roman warriors—" The leading guard went white.

Two hundred stayed in the stockade but eighty of us went through the narrow opening, stumbling over one another as we trampled the frightened Gauls in our path. We killed most of them, but a few got away. I heard cries and shouts and screams as those few raised the alarm.

Terence and I leaped back to avoid being crushed in the mad rush of escaping prisoners. "Tribune, how do we get out of this place to fight again?" one shouted joyfully.

"The horse herds of the Carthaginians lie beyond the last tent," Terence answered. He cupped his hands to his mouth; silence was no longer necessary. "Pick up stones! Anything you can find. If we're stopped, let's at least make a fight of it!"

Running back from where I had snatched up an enameled Carthaginian broadsword dropped by a dead Gaul, I told him, "Tribune, Varro was riding for the high road junction in Venusia!"

"We can make that if we have horses," Terence said. "Pass the word. Do it quickly!"

Our comrades spread out along the pen wall. In the starlight I ran from man to man, as Terence bade. Then, coming over a knoll I spied a large number of Hannibal's Spanish light infantry who were bivouacked nearby. The others saw them too, and panicked. I joined the mad, confused tide of men plunging toward the horse enclosures, and soon lost sight of the tribune who had arranged the rush out of the gates—

I caught a mount and hauled myself up. I kicked the animal without mercy and he broke into a run. I hung onto his mane, the wind whipping my face. The foothills at the end of the plain soon loomed ahead, a haven. Cries and the hoofbeats of the pursuers died for a while, and I believed I was safe, though separated from the rest, who had ridden or run in all directions. That is, those who had not been cut down by the Spaniards—

Without warning, the gods of luck turned their faces away from me. In a narrow and rocky watercourse, the mount I was riding stepped into a crack in the earth. As he fell, I heard the snap of his neck breaking.

The horse looked at me with great dumb eyes that shone in the ghostly glow of the stars. I cut his throat with a stroke to end his misery.

That is how I came to be left alone with but a cloak and a sword; alone in wild, unfamiliar country where every man might be my foe.

I took slow breaths, trying to compose myself. Rocky walls, lonely and desolate, rose all around.

I sighted by the stars and began to trudge. I would stay alive as long as the gods allowed—and rely on my wits as much as I relied on their fickle favor. As much, or more—

Soon parties of horseman began passing in the vicinity, but it was too dark and the terrain too tough for me to readily identify them. Each time I hid behind rocks until they were gone. Of course they might have been Romans, but they might just as easily have been Hannibal's bravos—and I did not intend to raise a hail and find out which.

# CHAPTER V

# AT THE FOUNTAIN
# OF DEATH

Four days later, shortly after dawn, on a morning heavy with mist, I stumbled into a small, poor village. The square of the town seemed deserted. I walked toward a fountain in the center, leaned over the rim and sloshed cool, sweet water over my head. Then I drank.

A shadow appeared. I glanced up. Three peasant men had emerged from the mist on the fountain's far side. Each man carried a stout staff. Exhausted as I was, I was still able to greet them:

"Brothers, the sight of you is good."

One of the citizens nudged another. "How is it that he speaks the language so well?"

"That devil Hannibal trains his spies and outriders in the tongue," was the reply.

"*Spies?* That's ludicrous. Be so kind as to tell me where I am—"

"It will do no good to feign ignorance," said the leader, a stocky, oafish-looking fellow. "This is the village of Chira in the district of Apulia, and well you know it. Your master has sent you into this land to take our grain and bread and to rape our women."

"That's right!" a new voice cackled. "Give the Carthaginian what he deserves."

"Carthaginian! You witless clods, I am a legionary! Linus Julius by name. Who spoke a moment ago?"

"I did!"

A spindly, vile-faced old shrew had appeared in front of me, along with perhaps a dozen townspeople. All of them were in angry temper. One of them apparently had seen me enter the square and had summoned the others. They crowded around, their faces gray in the mist. They were poor people. They looked ravaged by war, and tortured by the fear of more.

The oafish fellow spoke once again:

"If you are a Roman soldier, where is your armor? And why do you carry that kind of sword? No enamel worker in Latium ever crafted a hilt like that. But I saw a Carthaginian carrying such a sword."

He stepped closer, his small eyes brimming with animosity. "I speak of the Carthaginian who stripped my wife naked and violated her, while his men held me fast and looted my shop."

Now they were backing me against the fountain. I nearly went off balance as my elbow slipped in a niche in the fountain wall. A woman cried out. I jerked my head around to look—

Two yellow serpents were painted on the wall above this niche; the little recess contained a few coins. It

32

must have been the shrine of *lares compitalis,* the lesser gods of many a village crossroad.

"I swear to you," I exclaimed, "I am a soldier! Escaped four nights ago from Hannibal's prisoner pens at Cannae, near the shore of the sea."

"He's lying!" someone cried. "He's nothing but a Punic spy who lost his horse and threw away his fancy armor because he was afraid he'd be recognized."

An ugly muttering began and quickly grew louder. I heard shouts of "Pay the Carthaginian back for Claudio's death!" Soon the shouts rocked the square.

Vainly I tried arguing with them. They were afraid and finally confronted by an enemy whom they outnumbered. Besides, since I wore filthy bandages around my chest and no garment except a dirty cloak, they had no reason to believe me.

Yet, unless I thought of a way out, and quickly, it was likely they would tear me to pieces—

Hands picked up stones. "Remember what they did to Claudio!" the old hag cried, and flung hers.

"Get back, you damn fools," I yelled, raising my sword.

"Kill him!"

*"Stone him!"*

*"KILL THE PUNIC BUTCHER!"*

Rocks rained down. One of them struck me on the forehead. Another hit my side. The people had come closer and now surrounded me. The fountain was still at my back. There was no way to escape except by using my blade for the purpose of which it had been intended—to kill.

Another stone grazed my cheek. *"Kill him, strike the Carthaginian dead!"*

I raised my sword, deciding whom to hack at first—

33

*"Mad dogs! Get away from him!"*

Suddenly the stones ceased pelting me. The crowd parted. Incredibly, through a lane between the people there came, not some person of obvious authority, but a slim, dark-haired young girl.

She put down the water jar she carried, then pried a rock from the fat fingers of the oaf who had led this attack. She hurled the rock to the ground:

"What kind of hysteria possesses you, Gemmio?" she demanded. "Who started this? You? If I hadn't come into this village for water, as I usually do each morning, I suppose you would have killed him!"

Whoever she was, they seemed to listen to her. Fat Gemmio was positively craven:

"Nara, the man claims he's a Roman soldier. But he's plainly a Carthaginian who is lost. We were going to pay him back for Claudio. After all, Claudio was an important official here."

"He was also my brother!" Nara replied. "Did you forget that?"

"But the story that this man is a Roman is obviously a lie," Gemmio protested.

"Idiots—all of you! Idiots!" Nara cried. "Roman soldiers have been streaming through this district night and day."

Gemmio looked less certain. "No one has come through the village to my knowledge, Nara—"

"Since the high road runs high around the town, do you imagine they would? They're flying for their lives. Are you so sick with fear that you don't look beyond your own town square? Strangers pass on that high road and never know this village is here, hidden in hills—"

I wasted no time agreeing: "That's quite true. I lost my way after dark, and only stumbled across it."

"Don't listen to him—!" someone began.

"I tell you to leave him alone!" Nara said. "What if he is a Carthaginian? Will more killing bring Claudio back? Never. I'm certain this man is a legionary, just as he tells you. From my cottage near the high road, I have seen such men hurrying by, alone and in twos and threes. I've even fed some of them—while you have done nothing but hide under your beds waiting for one defenseless wretch to come along so that you can slake your hatreds. The gods help the Roman republic if she depends on the likes of you!"

By now Nara had slipped close to my side. I could see that she was not only of a bold temper, but pretty as well, with a supple form beneath her plain garments. Her high young breasts pushed in and out sharply as she watched the tense crowd. They might still decide to have at me—

"I don't know whether we'll get out of this," she whispered to me. "Or even whether you really are a Roman."

"I am," I told her softly. "However, if they don't choose to believe that, I'll use this sword to persuade them. I'll persuade a few of them into their graves, that I promise."

"No! You'll never have a chance if you start—"

"I say Nara is mistaken!" the fat Gemmio decided. "I say kill the man and ask questions later."

Needing only this leadership, the crowd assented. Gemmio hoisted up another rock:

"Stand off, Nara. Stand clear or you'll be hurt."

"They mean to do it," she breathed savagely. "Gods! Isn't there any way—?" She bit her full pink

35

lower lip, glancing over my shoulder at the village shrine.

"Watch out, Nara!" another man warned. She stood her ground. The first stone flew, narrowly missing my forehead.

Nara gripped my arm, her voice low and urgent:

"Fall to the ground at the next stone. Kick your heels. Scream. Don't question me—do it! It's our only chance!"

Another stone smacked the fountain. Another. Then half a dozen in a volley. "What madness—?" I began.

"*Do it* or we'll never leave this square alive!"

At last I believed I understood what she meant.

To an outsider it would have seemed a ludicrous performance. But to me it was deadly earnest. I stumbled to my knees and began to beat the earth, wailing for mercy.

Then I flopped over upon my back, gnashed my teeth and rolled my eyes. No one laughed.

The rocks stopped falling. I screamed nonsense, gibberish, spitting out words as I drummed my heels frantically on the ground.

"The gods from the shrine have possessed him!" Nara cried. "They've entered his body. Whether he's a Carthaginian or not, you don't dare touch a man whose person the gods have entered. Go to your houses! Or will you violate the rules of heaven as well as those of human charity?"

The old crone in the front of the crowd dropped her stone at last, covered her eyes and turned away, shuddering. I continued my performance, noticing from the corner of one eye that even the loud-mouthed Gemmio was pale. He spun—and ran. Within moments we were

36

the sole occupants of the square, she and I, two people alone in the morning mist.

She helped me up. Her fingers were warm and her skin smelled sweet and fresh, although her eyes were faintly bitter and by no means innocent, I thought.

"Are you a legionary in truth? Or do you come from Hannibal?"

"Both. My name is indeed Linus Julius. I escaped from Hanibal's prison pens."

When I gave her details of my rank, my position in the cavalry, and a bit of what I had seen at Cannae, she nodded her head and told me she believed me. Then and only then did she lead me across the square:

"My cottage lies this way. I can fix you a little broth. Is it true that the legions were defeated as badly as you say?"

"Worse than defeated, Nara. They were slaughtered. Only a few escaped."

"I wasn't telling the truth when I said I'd sheltered some of them, I only hoped it would be a useful lie. The soldiers waste no time stopping here. They keep to the high road, and they all seem to be heading in one direction. Almost running, some of them."

When I explained that the plebeian consul Varro hoped to rally the survivors of the disaster at the road junction, Nara shuddered and replied: "But if the battle was so terrible, what good will it do? Even if you fight again, can you stop Hannibal if he marches on Rome?"

"Very likely not." We were heading up the steep road out of the village. My shoulder had begun to ache dismally once again, as if the gore-encrusted wound had reopened. "But at least we can die honorably. Try

37

to erase some of the black marks left by our miserable performance of a few days ago—"

When we reached the crest of the hill, Nara pointed. "There is my cottage. Only a moment more and we will be—are you ill, soldier? Your face looks so white—"

"Nothing very bad," I muttered—by now thoroughly sick to my stomach, but not wanting to admit it to a woman. "Have the townpeople been ill-treated by Hannibal's men? They mentioned someone named Claudio who was killed—your brother, you said—"

"Aye. All the family I had left in the world. Claudio was one of the village elders. Punic outriders cut him down. That doesn't excuse what nearly happened a few moments ago, however. The people are frightened, and fear makes them foolish. Fear makes everyone foolish."

She paused as we neared the cottage and I was aware of her eyes studying me. "I saw Carthaginians riding by once, after daybreak. Now I remember that they were dark-fleshed men, not pale and wiry as you are—"

All at once, she averted her eyes. Then she hurried on to the cottage, as though she felt what I had felt also. We were man and woman, coming close to a thatched hut. The two of us would be alone there—

I rushed to catch up with her. The throb of my shoulder grew worse. Pain and fatigue quickly banished vague thoughts of dalliance, and put me in a black mood again:

"Fine treatment I got from those bumpkins back there—" I followed her inside. "But it's no worse than I almost got from one of my own comrades."

"What do you mean?"

Without precisely knowing why, I poured out the story of Pulvius's treachery. While I spoke, she set a cup of wine before me. Though it was poor stuff, I drank avidly. The drink and a mounting feverish feeling set my tongue to wagging. What I told her had been stored up a long time:

"Be born a common citizen, join up willingly when they draw your lot and what becomes of you? A nobleman tries to kill you! Then your own countrymen turn on you! And why did that fine, noble, General Hannibal spare me? Because he was reluctant to kill a soldier? Nonsense! To finance his military campaign, that's all. Honor's turned into a joke, love of country a lie—and courage—why—"

Without realizing it, I had gotten to my feet. "Courage is nothing more than the shortest route to catastrophe. I tell you this, girl. I've concluded there are only two things in this world in which a man can safely believe. Power. And riches. The consuls prated about the virtues of bravery and then led us to slaughter. Legion after legion—destroyed. Now understand me. Killing—facing death—a soldier expects that. It's his lot—but not when he's led to it like a dumb sheep, and has no chance. I swear to the gods that if I ever come out of this alive, I will never again believe any of those fine, lofty speeches from those who pretend to guide our destinies so wisely, so—bravely! They are liars. Rogues! A bunch of grasping vultures who—*who*—"

"Julius? What's wrong—?" She hurried to me. "Sit down again. You're trembling!"

"The rest of us in this world," I mumbled, "the common ones—we're merely dirt to be trampled on—"

39

Pain scorched in my wounds. The tiny cottage swam in flickering firelight. I caught one more sight of her looking at me with concern and then I fell over, senseless.

# CHAPTER VI

# NARA

Night darkened in the little room when I woke. I was stretched out on a narrow straw pallet. As I stirred, Nara turned from the hearth and walked toward me. Flames leaped from a sudden gust of wind outside. My clout still covered me, but the tight bandage around my chest was clean linen.

"There's a kettle of lentil soup on the fire, Julius. Would you like some?"

I managed to laugh. "Even more than the power and riches I remember ranting about."

She brought me an earthenware bowl, then drew up a stool while I ate. After a second bowl, I began to feel somewhat better.

"Thank you." I handed the bowl back. "Perhaps I had better take my cloak and start now. It's a distance yet to the junction, I imagine."

41

Nara's dark hair gleamed in the fire glow. "About a day on foot. You slept so soundly all of this day, I think you would profit by one more night of rest. Besides, it's raining a little. Listen to the wind."

I did. It was an eerie, forlorn sound. We were alone in a friendless night; a friendless world. I tried not to look at her but I could not help myself. Her body, her soft breasts beneath the deep blue wool of her gown, reminded me all too acutely that for many a long and weary month of campaigning, I had not so much as looked upon a comely woman.

"But I could travel a way yet tonight—"

She touched my hand. "Please don't. Since Claudio was killed, this cottage has been empty and grim. Just one evening. Tell me about yourself. Where you come from. I know it probably sounds foolish to you. But in time of war, with everything so uncertain, it isn't so wrong to want a little companionship, is it?"

There was a shine in her eyes; and it hinted of something else she could not struggle against—nor I.

"No, Nara. The gods cannot begrudge us that little. Don't take your hand away."

"I don't want you to think—I'm not a—a wanton woman, Julius." Her eyes clouded. "Although since Claudio was killed, I admit that I have thought I *could* be such, if that were the only means of leaving this place. It's no good to live by yourself. After a while you look out to see the bands of men racing by after dark and you wonder how soon the loneliness will destroy you—"

Her eyes filled with puzzled and unhappy tears. She squeezed my hand very hard.

"Come here, Nara," I said.

Without protest she rose and knelt down beside the pallet. I took her shoulders.

"We may have been friendless before we met today. Small people whom the great ones trample in their games of war and power. But tonight we needn't be lonely. Not tonight."

"No, Julius, we needn't." And she bent her soft mouth to mine.

As she knelt beside me, her lips were sweet, yielding, gentle at first. Then, shyly, one of her hands touched the back of my neck.

Soon, with a soft, almost frightened little moan she pressed her mouth deeply to mine and opened her lips.

I lifted her up beside me. The flesh of her shoulders grew warm as I helped her with the garments. All at once it was no longer a matter of who was the aggressor, for her mouth turned hot and her breathing grew fast with desire. She guided my hands to her round, firm breasts.

At last both of us lay side by side. For a moment we did not touch each other. Then her legs pressed mine as though she sought to draw heat out of them, to store up against lonely days ahead. She buried her mouth against my neck. We caressed with mounting eagerness—

"I know you don't love me, Julius. Only—just pretend. For this one night, pretend that you do."

And who is to say, for that night alone, that I didn't love her? We needed each other, and that is the first step. Need often deepens into affection and then, perhaps, into love. The love can last a lifetime or vanish in an hour, but let no man deny its strength while it is there. Let no man say that the love does not exist; that

43

the love is hollow; that it is a sham or mockery. At such a time it is not.

The night passed, first in a frenzy and then with quiet, calm pleasure. It was more different this time than at any I could remember in the past. She had great lust but she had great sweetness too. She had passion, but she was far more than a vessel to be used. We were lovers, but we were also friends—

I awoke to find her already dressed. It was dawn. She smiled at me as she stirred the kettle:

"Somehow gruel seems like a banquet this morning—"

She brought me a steaming bowl as she had done last night. Again she took up her stool. Rain still fell on the thatched roof. Lightly, she touched my chin:

"When I opened my eyes, I felt finer than I have in many a month. But I'm afraid I did you no service. That bandage around your chest is changed again— had you noticed? The wound broke during the night."

"For a worthy cause, anyway."

She laughed at that.

"The rain sounds heavy."

"Too heavy for journeying. Julius, will you stay one more day?"

"Yes, of course. But I must definitely leave when the rain breaks."

Her fingers tightened on mine. "This place has grown so dismal without my brother—" Suddenly she leaned forward. "When you go, take me with you to Rome!"

"How can I do that? I have no idea where the army will go—if there is an army left."

"Certainly you'll go to Rome to defend that city.

44

You said so yourself—" She laughed. "—on one of the few occasions when we talked during the night."

I paid no heed to the joke; she'd raised a serious issue:

"Nara, Rome is a wretched town for the poor. You'd be no better off than here, and perhaps worse. Rome's crowded, dirty, and in a terrible state because of the war. What would you do there?"

"Anything," she replied simply. Gone was all her shyness, replaced by an almost brutal practicality that I did not like one bit. "Anything to earn my place and be rid of this lonesome house and this wretched life."

"When you say anything," I replied as I ate, "you have no idea what you mean. The word *anything* related to Rome covers a variety of vices, none of which you would care to indulge in."

"Talking like a husband already!" she said tartly. "I mean it, though. I want to leave this place and all its bad memories. I would even sell myself in exchange for the safety of the capital. There are worse things than doing that, you know—"

I was astonished and disgusted: "You would become a whore?"

"What is worth more to you?" she countered, almost angry. "Life, or your so-called honor? You said yourself that honor is a lie."

"I know, I know. Still, for a girl like you—"

I shook my head, unable to make clear in my own head what it was that I wanted to say.

"Don't sentimentalize with me, Julius. In another age—in a peaceful time—I might think otherwise. But my brother's death went hard with me. He was all the family I had in this world. I want to escape this hut and its memories in any way that I can!"

45

I must have sounded unbearably pompous when I said, "The idea you propose makes me sick."

She laughed again, rather harshly. "You mean the idea of my going to Rome?"

"No, the other. The means you'd take to support yourself."

Warned by the flicker of anger in her dark eyes, I told her truthfully: "Though I suppose I can't blame you for saying it. Certainly many a wench from the country has a prosperous life that way. But Gods! At what a price! It's despicable that a girl like you must even think about such things—"

I bent my head over the warm bowl. "I don't want to talk about it anymore—"

Quietly: "But we must. Until you answer my question. Will you take me?"

"And be responsible for what happens to you? I couldn't do that—"

"Julius, *I'm* the one suggesting it."

"*Enough!*" I flung the bowl away. I rose from the pallet finding myself not as weary as I had thought I would be. I pulled on a threadbare blanket tunic, once her brother's, which she had found for me earlier. Then I donned my cloak and stalked outside to stare at the country hills and the falling rain.

Had I so deluded myself by Nara's lovemaking last night that I believed one tumble in the dark could change the nature of things? Of course if she went to Rome—and the idea was in some ways eminently sensible—she would have to support herself as best she could. Prostitution was hardly more shameful than many of the practices of the greedy and debauched patricians. In one sense even more honorable, since it was at least straightforward—

46

Yet caught between the Nara who had been in my arms and the Nara who thought of whoredom, I remained confused and angry.

Fortunately she didn't raise the subject the rest of the day. When the rain stopped near dusk and she sent me out across the hillside fields to gather a few melons, I had still given her no answer. I was agonizing over her request when a scream tore through the lowering dusk.

I whirled and plunged back down the hill. Well before I reached the open cottage door, I saw what was happening inside. Two men were struggling with her. Glimmering white skin told me that she had been stripped naked.

Again the scream tore out. My belly tightened and grew cold as I saw a flash of armor and knew the identity of the two who were trying to rape her—

They were men who had passed on the highroad, and decided to stop.

They were Roman soldiers.

# CHAPTER VII

## SOLDIER'S REWARD

"Be sweet to us, dove. Be sweet or we'll be rough—
Oh! The bitch! Hold her, Quinux—tightly!"

The bigger of the legionnaires inside the cottage had
bellowed a stream of such orders, alternately laughing
and cursing while the two of them struggled with Nara.
Her hair had come unpinned and flew around her
shoulders in a dark veil as she twisted, bit and clawed
at them. The bigger man was also the younger and
stronger-looking, I saw as I raced nearer to the door.

Nara broke loose from them. She fetched the other
soldier, Quinux, a savage blow across the cheek. He
was ugly in body and face, a short, bandy-legged sort
in tarnished greaves. His fat whey face had only one
good eye, the other being a black, puckered slit.

I was nearly to the cottage now. I saw that they had
a single mount between them, a runty pony, no doubt

stolen. The fat legionary dived for Nara. There was blood on his jaw. He was shouting:

"—teach you to treat a Roman soldier that way. One who nearly got his guts hacked out at Cannae. Fought for you, and now you—*damn it, put that down!*"

With a brutal blow of his hand Quinus, the one-eyed, struck at her wrist while the taller one laughed uproariously. The firebrand from the hearth fell from Nara's fingers. At that instant, I snatched a rock from the ground and rushed inside.

"Turn around, you jackals!"

The bigger one squinted at me. Then laughed again. He was wearing a sword, worse luck. "Well! What kind of strutting country chicken is this? Are you the lady's lover, fellow? If so, just stand back and wait until we're finished. We're only taking our just reward as soldiers."

On the earthen floor a goatskin of wine had spilled some of its red contents. Perhaps the wine accounted for the big legionary's blurry speech and for the sickly-sweet miasma of drunkenness in the cottage. Nara breathed hard, her eyes large and round. Her nude breasts were white and shaking with fright.

"You'll get your reward when the tribunes catch hold of you," I said to them. "I came from the same field as you—Cannae. My name is Linus Julius. I was *praefectus equitum* of the Ninth. Perhaps we wouldn't have lost the battle if we'd had more men and fewer dogs who attack women for a pastime."

The one-eyed Quinux began to tremble. "He's lying, Polidor. He has no sword—no armor—"

"Trifles," said Polidor wearily. "If he's what he says he is, and he reports us, we're done."

The tall legionary was sober in a second. He smiled

50

in a disarming way, then added, "If he ever reports us."

Rape was no light crime for a legionary. Still I didn't quite count on such an overwhelming lack of loyalty. He shrugged to Quinux as if to say that the matter was ended. He reached down for his fallen helmet. The jerk of his back as he straightened warned me too late—

The helmet flew at me, striking me hard on the face. I stumbled backwards. Polidor shouted, "On to him, Quinux! We can't leave a witness."

I crashed against the shaky cottage wall. The big legionary's blade slid free, a bright white glare in the light of the fireplace. That blade seemed to be racing at me, to be growing wider and longer as its point was driven toward my throat.

Desperately I hurled myself to the side. Polidor cursed. He found himself stabbing empty air.

The force of his thrust carried him half through the door, but only half. I scrambled for the rock I had dropped, then spun and flung it at his head. Polidor screamed when it struck him. His nose was shattered, and in a moment it was leaking blood.

"The little one!" Nara cried behind me.

Then Quinux was on me like a nagging dog. His fat fingers dug into my throat. He was hanging onto my back, panting.

Polidor lurched at us, grinning nastily now. Quinux held me tightly enough for Polidor to have a chance at his target. "Hold him a moment more," Polidor panted, drawing back his sword arm—

Suddenly a hissing sheet of boiling water descended on him. He dropped his sword and clapped both hands to his face, shrieking again. Nara let go of the water kettle she'd pulled from the fire hook to douse him,

51

and I smashed Quinox's belly with my elbow. When he grunted and dropped off of my back, I went at Polidor.

The big man's face was burnt raw by the scalding water. He hadn't stopped screaming, but he managed to snatch up his sword. Something else winked bright—I lifted my hand to catch the crude dagger tossed to me; she must have kept it near the fire for preparing food. Polidor came on, stumbling like some injured giant, chopping back and forth in the air with his blade and mouthing obscene oaths—

I ducked in time to avoid a swipe of the blade that would have taken my head off. Then I rose and jammed the dagger through a joint in Polidor's armor, directly into his heart.

I jerked my head back, and myself as well. Blood was spraying like a fountain. In that light it seemed to be various shades of red. Polidor's tongue, another shade of red, protruded. His eyes bulged as he toppled.

Breathing hard, I wiped my face. "Where's the other one?"

Nara rushed to me, her nakedness cold in the crook of my arm. "Gone. He ran away—"

Down toward the high road the rattling hoofs of their flea-bitten mount died out. I stared at the hideous corpse on the wine-and blood-soaked earth, and buried my face in the curve of Nara's neck. In that way, almost unbidden, the decision came to me. This cottage was accursed now. I couldn't leave her to smell old blood forever, until the day she died.

"We must bury him, Nara. Bury him deeply and well, before we leave this place together."

# CHAPTER VIII

# *REUNION*

After moonrise, with Polidor under the ground and the cottage stripped of its few possessions, and these wrapped in a bundle, Nara and I took the high road for the junction. At one point she asked me what would happen if the killing were ever discovered. I told her it would not go easy with me, even though Polidor deserved his fate. The sole witness was that one-eyed man, Quinux. The slim chance of encountering him again was a risk I had no choice but to accept.

During the night we passed and were passed by bands of soldiers all scurrying in the same direction. None of them molested us. I soon grew so weary of walking that I abandoned my worries over the fate to which I might be leading Nara as a result of my decision. She, on the other hand, seemed to consider this whole journey as a sort of lark, which didn't help my spirits at all.

By nightfall next day, we saw torches burning on the horizon. We reached the great junction of the two highroads and in the adjacent meadows discovered a rude camp. Legionnaires stared at us listlessly as we sought the commander's standard. The scene was one of sadness and desolation. There were several thousand who had rejoined Varro—ten thousand, I later learned—yet they hardly resembled a Roman fighting force. The men were silent and sullen. Suspicious eyes reflecting torchlight watched our every step.

"There," I pointed. "Yonder on the hill. That tent must be Varro's."

So it was. As we neared it, I heard a kind of drunken ranting from inside. The centurion who barred our path at the entrance said:

"Try to find your unit. No one is to be admitted tonight. The consul is—indisposed."

"Indisposed or not, I have urgent news which he may not have received yet. Stand aside."

He could not be sure of my rank. But I must have looked determined, for he hesitated only a moment, then drew the hanging away.

"Don't leave this man's side until I come out," I told Nara. "You're my responsibility now, remember." So saying, I went inside. There, by the light of an oil lamp, Gaius Terentius Varro was getting drunk.

I saluted and identified myself. The butcher's son who had gained his office because of lately earned wealth and windbag oratory glared at me from his couch. Wine spotted his tunic. Gray, flabby cheeks and forehead shone with sweat and ringlet oil. What I saw in his small and muddy eyes was hardly human. It was animal fear.

Varro waved listlessly. "Ordinary soldiers report to their unit, not to me." He lifted a wine jar. "That is, if the unit can be found in this dismal camp—"

"May the honorable consul forgive me for interrupting, but I have news that may be important."

"I know the news," he replied, seeming to stare straight through me. "Varro bungled. Varro is a fool. Varro should be stripped of his rank." His voice rose. "It wasn't my fault! The legions must be told that Hannibal's cleverness can only be overcome by an army not twice the size of his, but ten times the size. *Twenty times!* The Senate must be told this as well. It—" his voice broke, and for a moment he looked more child than man. "It wasn't my fault. We have only ten thousand left here. No more are coming. Ten thousand to fight forty. Impossible odds. We will lose."

"There'll be more swords available if the Thunderbolt has his way," I said to him. "While I was a prisoner at Cannae, Hannibal himself told me the rest of those captured would be ransomed at so much per head." Quickly I explained the circumstances of how I'd learned this. "I disturbed the consul only because I thought perhaps he hadn't heard of the ransom plan—"

Varro wiped his nose with his tunic sleeve. "No, I have not. No messenger has reached me here. Surely it's another scheme. A deception—and they'll blame me for this one, too!" Abruptly his head lifted. His lips wrenched. "Well, don't stand there accusing me like all the rest! You've delivered your message. Get out and leave me in peace!"

And he flung the wine jar across the tent.

It spilled at my feet, gurgling softly. Varro studied it like a man demented. Then he rolled over on his couch, showing me his back. A shudder ran up my spine as I spun and fled. To hear a grown man crying is an unnerving experience.

Outside, I seized Nara's arm:

"Let's get away from this place. I think the gods may have cursed that coward in there. Perhaps the rout wasn't entirely his fault after all."

For the better part of an hour we searched the hillside for familiar faces. A few lustful looks came Nara's way, but since several large groups of noisy peasant women had found their way to the function, the girl at my side aroused only minimal attention. At last, by one campfire, I sighted a familiar and finely cut profile, brooding over red embers.

"Tribune? *Terence?* It *is* you—!"

Octavius Terence leaped up. "By the immortals! My companion from the pens."

We embraced like long-separated brothers, and relief swept over me, for while I had not known him long, there was something about him that inspired trust and respect.

I introduced Nara, who finally showed signs of growing weary from our long trip on foot. Terence bowed with a brand of politeness and grace that immediately stamped him once again as an aristocrat. He gestured beyond the circle of drowsy men:

"Do you see that thick tree bole yonder? A good place for resting. Here, take my cloak and settle yourself. You'll be perfectly safe. Julius and I will sit awhile and talk."

Nara smiled sleepily. "Thank you, Tribune." She touched my hand, then left us. After we had watched her settle herself and arrange the cloak, Teretius said softly:

"Far be it from me to criticize, Julius, but is such extra baggage a wise burden?"

"There was no choice." We took places beside the fire. Lowering my voice, I told him of killing Polidor. He never commented on it, except to nod once or twice as if suggesting that in the circumstances, I had been bound to bring her. I finished:

"What worries me most is what will become of her when we reach Rome."

"Fret over that if we *do* get there. Considering Varro's state, I doubt we will. Who knows where an army will end up when it's commanded by a man whose mind has been unhinged by a defeat he knows to be his own doing? They issued a food ration this morning, but no wine. Some say there isn't any. Some say Varro drinks it all."

Up in black treetops a bird hooted, an eerie, lonesome sound. Memory nagged me.

"Terence, have you seen a one-eyed soldier anywhere about? A little, stumpy man—?"

He said he had not.

"Then what of the master of the horse?"

The tribune's eyes met mine, somber. "Sardus Pulvius? The one you told me about that night in the pens? For your sake I'm glad to say I've seen no sign of him."

"That's good news. The last I knew, he rode away with Varro. Perhaps he was killed."

"Perhaps. Let's hope it happened. You're not pleasant to look at when you speak of him."

"Why should I look pleasant? He tried to kill me because he took a tumble during a horse race he himself arranged! He's the one responsible for my having Nara on my hands, not to mention a dead soldier on my conscience. Everything I've been through I owe to him—including the disgusting spectacle of Roman citizens turning on me like I was some kind of predator. I tell you, Terence, it's a filthy world if men and women attack their own kind and a girl like Nara says that she's willing to become a whore to be safe in the capital—"

Terence's gray eyebrows quirked up. "That is her plan for supporting herself?"

"It is unless I can prevent her. I must."

"Are you in love with this girl?"

"No, but she is my responsibility. Isn't that nearly the same thing?"

Angrily, I flung a handful of twigs into the fire. Sparks shot up to the lightless sky. "What kind of a world is it when every single day brings worry and fear but never any relief?"

"Reading the philosophical books—though hardly a practical pastime for a soldier—teaches one thing, Julius. Namely, the world doesn't change. It is the same now as it was when Troy fell and even before. It will surely be the same world long after both of us are dead. But you are young, comparatively, and are just having the first taste of the behavior of men like Pulvius and Varro and that soldier you killed. I know ideals die hard"

"And are very foolish. They're the baubles with which idiots delude themselves."

"Not so—or not completely so, anyway. The man who would not lose his mind in this world is the man who knows his inevitable lot is hardship, danger, fear—and ultimately—death. But the man knows something else too. He knows that now and again, honor shines through for a moment. Or love. Or friendship. Such moments can't be destroyed by all the Varros in creation. Those moments alone make life bearable. When they come, it is a blessing and a balm."

He saw I was unconvinced, so he clapped me on the shoulder and rose:

"Well, enough maundering. It's time we slept. There's talk of marching to Rome when the sun reaches noon tomorrow. Pray to the gods that we don't find Hannibal's host drawn up ahead of us."

He wandered off among the sleeping men, sank down and soon closed his eyes. I remained long by the fire, still doubting his words about honor and friendship and love. In that dismal camp, such notions seemed as remote as the moon, and fully as irrelevant.

# CHAPTER IX

# HERO'S WELCOME

The hills beside the winding, mud-brown Tiber flashed in the sun some days afterward, their great golden buildings creating a luminous yellow haze on the horizon. Thousands of us marched in ragged file along the Via Sacra. Varro rode a spindly white horse at the head of the column. I was close behind him with the officers, but there was no semblance of organization.

I started when I heard the messenger cry, "Where is the Prefect Linus Julius? Forward at once! Consul Varro wishes to present you. Hurry, man!"

Following the messenger rather unsteadily, I came to a party of noblemen drawn up before the head of the column. Astride a fine mount, his creamy purple-edged toga spotless, sat the paunchy, wart-faced old man who guided the destinies of Rome. The dictator Quintus Fabius.

He looked more a schoolmaster than a warrior, and indeed, many had grumbled that he behaved like a schoolmaster when commanding an army. Near him, Varro appeared relatively sober. But I saw sweat on his cheeks.

"*Ave,* Excellency!" I greeted, somewhat awed by the great man's presence.

"*Ave,* Linus Julius!" Fabius replied. "Consul Varro has just informed me that you brought him word of a plan Hannibal Barca has proposed for ransoming our soldiers."

"That is true, sir. But he did not say how or when the ransoming would be accomplished."

Fabius smiled, displaying bad teeth. "Well, I have no quarrel with a ransom—nor any quarrel with the army's performance. You fought hard and valiantly, so the reports relate. I came out here to offer you my commendation, and a welcome home—"

At that, Varro looked as if he'd faint in the saddle. His obvious relief was almost pathetic. Fabius continued:

"Prefect, explain how you came to learn of Hannibal's willingness to ransom back our men."

Only just launched into the narrative, I was cut off by the appearance of another party of horsemen. This band was headed by a spindly, long-lawed old nobleman who sat well in spite of his mount's high spirits. He returned the hails of Varro and the rest with a curt, grumpy one of his own.

"Honorable Torquatus," said Fabius amiably, "what brings you out of the walls?"

"News of the arrival of this company of cowards." The old man fingered his white beard. "Do you mean to say you intend to let the consul here return in honor?"

This time Varro nearly did fall from the saddle, so sudden was his reversal of fortune. Fabius scowled:

"Remember your place, Torquatus. Though you've served Rome well in the field, and are today a senator, these men have borne the brunt of Cannae. They've returned to fight for the Republic again. They are to be welcomed, not condemned. There is even the possibility that we might have more swords to aid them before long—"

The dictator pointed me out by name and described the ransom plan, commenting, "The idea strikes me as most sensible. To preserve those city walls, every man is needed. I'm sure the Senate will appropriate necessary funds—"

Seated on his nervous mount, Torquatus snorted almost as loudly as the animal. "Not while my voice can be heard! I won't vote to spend one denarius!" He glared at Varro again. "The soldiers who survived Cannae were cowards, unwilling to fight and die at the end. Don't tell me otherwise—I've already heard the accounts of the battle. I won't take part in this mockery, Fabius. Furthermore, I'll argue with my last breath against honoring these men. Their presence here isn't a sign of heroism, only proof that they ran away."

"To fight again for our city!" Varro exclaimed almost hysterically.

"*No!*" Torquatus thundered. "To be *safe* from fighting. To save your wretched lives! It's an insult to Rome to call you heroes. If you're heroes, you're Hannibal's, not ours!"

And he wheeled his horse and led his followers back toward the city.

Varro swayed in the saddle. Fabius frowned at me. "Dismissed, Prefect, dismissed!" As I left, he began conferring hastily with the consul.

When I rejoined the officers, the Tribune Terence explained the reasons for the strange scene:

"Years ago, Torquatus distinguished himself with the legions in Cisalpine Gaul. He's one of those blighted men who thinks war is glorious, always glorious. But I suspect the real reason for his animosity is the fact that he leads a sizeable Senate faction opposed to Varro. Torquatus was defeated for consular office by Varro in the last election. So the senator obviously intends to stir up trouble against us—" He shook his head. "Not good."

Presently trumpets sounded. The column advanced into the city. A crowd had turned out. A few cheered, but most were silent and scornful. Then I heard someone cry: "There go Hannibal's heroes!"

Laughter swirled around us, and I knew Terence's prophecy of bad times ahead was accurate. Ten thousand had marched back to fight, and in one hour that effort had been turned into a mockery.

The ten thousand from Cannae went into temporary quarters in a huge, wood-palisaded tent city in the lower slope of the Pincian hill overlooking the camp of the Praetorian guards.

For several days we never left that enclosure. We were busy with the digging of drainage ditches, the staking out of streets and the refurbishing of the pitifully small amount of equipment left to us. Through Fabius's offices, however, we were eventually supplied with new armor from the storehouses. But there were no animals to be had for cavalrymen like me, so I found myself a foot soldier with a temporary rank of sub-centurion in charge of a maniple, the units making up the larger cohorts. Impatiently through all this, I waited for an opportunity to slip out of camp and see to Nara's well-being.

I had sent her to an innkeeper in the field of Mars. The man had known my deceased uncle well. In my message to the landlord, I promised to pay for Nara's keep, and he sent back a note saying that he would put her to work to earn part of it until I arrived.

A week passed before I was able to get away at night. During that week, the situation in Rome lowered the spirits of every man, even though we got our news only secondhand from outside the camp's log walls:

Hannibal's victorious host had turned aside to Capua and not marched upon Rome after all. Rumor said that his sub-commanders had argued for a lightning strike against the practically defenseless capital. But Hannibal wished to keep his troops out of another major battle for a while. Since crossing the Alps, they had been two years in the field.

His decision, if we were able to read it properly, relieved the tension in the city of the seven hills only partially. Rome still effectively lacked an army.

Quintus Fabius quickly took charge and made the best of the situation. Martial law was declared and enforced by the Praetorians. Guards blocked every city gate. Citizens were not allowed out. A curfew governed the comings and goings of all those except soldiers. To justify these measures, Fabius read the sacred Sibylline Book of Fates almost daily and issued proclamations saying the situation called for extraordinary and heroic sacrifices on the part of the populace.

Two cohorts were brought in from the port of Ostia

as reinforcements. Prisoners and slave pens were thrown open. Bands of men went from house to house, from temple to temple, collecting every horse, every bit of precious metal to be found. Soon two legions of slaves and convicts were countermarching and drilling on the Praetorians' grounds. Mothers frightened their children by telling them that Hannibal was at the gate. A slogan scrawled in charcoal appeared on walls all over the city:

*Hannibal's Heroes placed their own lives above Rome.*

Given the state of the world as I saw it, such insults to soldiers who had tried to do the right thing didn't surprise me. Besides, I was more concerned about Nara. After that first week elapsed, a paymaster finally appeared with our purses. Mine, including field pay, totaled about 75 denarii. And I was able to gain permission to leave the camp at night and hurry through the dark silent streets.

Along the arcades in the Campus Martius I came to the old, wine-fragrant inn of Castor and Pollux. The innkeeper, a swarthy, good-natured fellow, no longer considered me a friend:

"Put up your cloak hood, Julius. My patrons have been in an ugly mood lately."

I indicated the walls where someone had chalked, *Hannibal's Heroes have yellow backs.* "Over that nonsense?"

"It's not nonsense, it's the mood of everyone from mighty Torquatus on down."

"Yes, I know all about it," I said, disgusted. "Here is the fee I promised you. Where is the wench?"

"In the back, scrubbing. I told you I'd put her to work. She won't last long in the tavern trade, Julius.

She has grander ideas. I advise you to get her out of here. I want no trouble."

And with that he rushed over to a table where several patrons were staring at me in an unpleasant way. The landlord began trying to pacify them with a bawdy story. Irked, I went down the passage to the kitchen.

Nara was on her knees with a water tub and cloth, polishing the stones. Her hair hung over her forehead. Her *palla* was stained in many places. She looked tired and bitter.

"I would have come sooner," I explained, "but they kept us busy in camp."

"And I would have been gone from here," she blazed back, "except that I felt obliged to wait and tell you."

Her scowl disturbed me. "Tell me what?"

"That I don't intend to stay in this miserable den, working on my knees."

Angrily I gripped her arm. "Nara, I warned you that life in Rome wouldn't be easy—"

"Don't worry, it will be easy enough in another kind of work!"

So saying, she returned to her labor. There was nothing for me to do but take my leave, heavy-hearted with the knowledge that my promise of finding her a better life had been an empty one.

The problem weighed on my mind during the next week when events took another drastic turn:

A new military commander of whom I had heard took charge of the two freshly recruited legions of criminals and debtors. They were slated to march into the field soon. That left the fate of our ten thousand still undecided. But a hint of it came every time we passed the open gates of our camp. Vendors outside jeered and pointed:

"Hannibal's Heroes! Hannibal's Heroes!" They flung dirt and stones and offal, and ran away laughing.

Tempers grew short. Fights broke out in camp. Torquatus and his faction must have been busy. We lived beneath a deepening cloud of shame.

Then an emissary arrived at Rome from Hannibal's camp somewhere in the north. But we heard of it only after the emissary had been turned back at the Alban hills by one of Fabius's lictors. The dictator refused to entertain the Carthaginian's plea for a peace parley, and denied the man entrance to the city.

Accompanying the Carthaginian had been ten legionnaires, hostages pledged to return to Hannibal's camp with or without the ransom fund. The hostages had to be locked up under guard in Rome for they were not safe in the open, being considered worse traitors than we were held to be.

Talk spread that a hot debate on the question of the ransom was to be held in the Senate shortly. There was no doubt in anyone's mind that Torquatus would speak against the idea. How Fabius would react was an imponderable, but our fate was certainly linked to his power—or to his lack of it. We all knew that very well.

# CHAPTER X

# "A WHORE BORN AND BRED"

Yet even all these worries seemed petty next to my constant concern about Nara. I made some inquiries on her behalf, but Rome was flooded with refugees and work simply did not exist for an untrained country girl such as she was. It was this news that I reported with a heavy heart when I returned to the inn of Castor and Pollux on one nasty, drizzling night.

Curiously, Nara seemed unaffected:

"Don't fret about it, Julius. Since that new army everyone is talking about—what's the commander's name? Marcellus?—has been formed, people seem to be visiting this place in great numbers. Perhaps fears have relaxed a little. At least the tavern keeper tells me so. The work is not quite so unbearable as it was."

She patted my cheek as though I were a fretful, foolish child. By the light of the cheap brass lamp in her room under the eaves, I tried to read her strange smile.

"Then just have patience a while longer, Nara. If things do improve—"

She threw her arms around me. "Didn't I say they're improving already? I feel good this evening, Julius. It's cozy in here with the rain beating down." She pressed her mouth to mine suddenly.

In a moment, I was letting my confusion and uncertainty drown in kisses and caresses. On her pallet she drew off her gown and smiled, her nude flesh shining softly. There was a strange kind of enigmatic quality haunting her eyes that night. When I stretched beside her, to caress her breasts and her trembling legs, she gave little passionate cries and was nimble, almost frantic, as we made love.

There was little joy in it, though. In truth, her behavior seemed mechanical and forced. It was almost as if I was making love to a girl I had never known before; a girl who was—or wanted to be—experienced.

Bracing herself on her elbows afterwards, the tender pink ends of her breasts gleaming in the lamplight, she stared at me and asked:

"Will I do, Julius? Am I practiced enough?"

"What the devil are you talking about?"

"I said there was no need to worry over me. With the clientele picking up, I've made the acquaintance of one or two patrons of good families. Pleasant, kindly men—"

I grabbed her wrists. "Do you mean to say that you've already turned yourself into a whore?"

"I am turning myself into a *free person*!" She wrenched away. "Not dependent on a man like you. Oh, Julius, I'm not doing it because I dislike you! Just

70

the opposite. I am more than fond of you." Brief sadness in her eyes; then her smile turned rueful. "But you're a soldier. You have no time for women—"

Her face changed again, hardening. "That's why I must go my own way. I don't intend to drudge in this place forever. Besides, I don't think you love me—nor do I expect you to, really—"

It seemed she knew me better than I knew myself. I cursed the fate that made me so damnably scrupulous that I couldn't bring myself to lie to her, or to pretend love when there was none in me. But I argued with her; pleaded. It was fruitless:

"No, you can't change my mind. Nor should you worry about doing so." Again she stretched on her pallet, luxuriously opening her arms. "But I'll always be grateful to you, my dear. Come here again and let me demonstrate—"

She reached down to pat the soft, smooth whiteness of her belly. In that moment I saw not a peasant girl but a mannered, simpering courtesan. What she was becoming, I had made her. With a curse, I stumbled up, seized my cloak and rushed out. A sound that might have been a sob but could have easily have been a laugh followed me down the stairs.

Unpleasant looks flashed at me from the customers. The innkeeper didn't enjoy filling my order for a pot of wine, but I slammed down my coins and scowled at him and he had no choice.

While I was staring into the dregs, I became conscious of someone watching me.

Slowly, I swung around. A spindly fellow who had teeth like a horse hastily averted his eyes. I continued to stare. Through the wine fumes came the certainty

71

that I had seen the fellow lounging about the premises on my previous visit.

And his stare was too intense for mere curiosity. When he caught me continuing to watch him, he flushed. Quickly he threw down a coin and walked toward the door. I rose to follow. "Good riddance to a coward," one of the patrons muttered.

In the street, I ran after the spindly man, up along slops-strewn cobbles between closely built houses. A distant torch in a niche threw weird lights on the wet stone under foot. The man's footfalls ran out hollow ahead.

"You there—hold up!" I shouted, lengthening my stride. He spun around, bolting into an alleyway. By the time I reached it, his running feet had carried him out of my sight.

I leaned into the protection of a wall, then tightened my helmet strap and frowned into the rain. Perhaps it was only an armor thief. Bands of them roamed at night. Yet I could not help but think that the fellow had known me, and that he had watched me for a purpose. What the purpose was, I couldn't say. I shrugged it off and tried to forget it.

"Ah, roistering?" Terence the tribune said when I entered the tent a short while later. The other four officers were rolled up in their blankets, asleep. "I have been waiting for you, my friend."

In the rainy darkness, the chill air, that last word had a good sound. I realized that he was indeed a friend. We were not alike, Terence and I, but perhaps we balanced one another. At any rate, as I threw off my damp wool cloak, friendship seemed a welcome commodity.

"Not roistering exactly," I told him. My cheeks had

become shamefully hot. "I've been looking after Nara. Badly, as it's turned out."

"Well, I'll be happy to lend an ear to your domestic problems, Julius, but first hear the news I've been waiting to tell you. How is your speaking ability?"

I blinked. "Poor. I'm a soldier, not an orator."

"But an orator is what you will be very soon."

"What the devil are you talking about?"

"You recall that the Senate plans to hold a public hearing on whether to pay Hannibal's ransom demands and free our brethren whom he still holds in captivity somewhere up north. Well, several of us from Cannae have been selected to speak to the Conscript Fathers and explain our side of that engagement. It's Varro's doing, I think. His reputation depends upon convincing the Senate of the inability of the legions—outnumbered at the end of the battle, and outfought—to do anything but surrender. I know you've also seen the slogans. Those of us chosen to speak must try to wipe them out by what we say."

"This is folly!" I told him. "I won't do it."

"You have no choice."

"But I have no education, either—no skill with words—"

Terence shrugged. "I can only assume that Varro put your name up because you heard the ransom offer from Hannibal in person. I assure you there's no avoiding the assignment. The roster has been posted. The hearing will take place a week from today, and I wouldn't take it lightly—" His voice was grave. "Our words may decide whether those Romans still in chains go to the slave dealers of Delos, or go free. But our future is in the balance too. Now, with that news delivered, what is happening between you and Nara?"

73

"Nothing that oratory will solve," I complained. "Let us not talk about it. I'm out of the mood. Gods! Speech-making in the Senate—!"

Over and over in the succeeding days, I rehearsed what I would say. As the time for the hearing approached, new trouble struck. I became aware when I went to answer a summons from the innkeeper:

"I am going to have to turn the wench out, Master Julius. She isn't earning her keep. She's taken to slipping out at all hours of the night, she goes about the place wearing embroidered *stolae* and *pallae* that she never owned when she came here."

I stared into his plain face and saw that he wasn't lying. Which meant the worst had happened. She was selling herself, exactly as she'd threatened to do.

"She doesn't know what she's doing," I said. "She'll be badly used. I must prevent that. Stop her before some misbegotten nobleman makes a demand she won't be able to bring herself to satisfy. You know what patricians do to whores that refuse them anything—"

The man shuddered. "Yes, I've seen a few of the girls like that afterward. But what can I do? I'm not her keeper."

Desperate, I pulled out my meager purse. "Let me hire your sweeping boy to follow her. To learn where she goes. Before I accuse her, I must discover the names of a few of her customers. I can find out about them by speaking to some of the officers who were raised here in Rome. Then perhaps I can give her a more accurate picture of what she's letting herself in for. I'll try to show her these men have cast other women aside when they've finished with them, and the women have always been the worse for it—"

I pressed money into his palm. "You must help me this last time."

He sighed. "Frankly, I think she's a whore born and bred. But because of the friendship I once bore for your uncle, who was a fine man, I will."

He called the sweeping boy who was dozing in a corner. We gave him instructions. The boy snatched my money and nodded:

"Tomorrow, then, I will try to see where she wanders after dark, and I'll report back."

"What's wrong with tonight?" I demanded.

"Why, sir," he said, grinning a lewd grin that froze my heart, "not two hours ago I saw her creep from the kitchen to the passage outside. A fine litter was waiting. The lady's already gone out to practice her trade."

And like some obscene little animal, his knowing eyes mocking me for the fool I probably was, he tucked the coins away in a deep pocket and went back to sleep by the fire.

# CHAPTER XI

# RIOT

"Consul! Consul! Consul!"

The shout was begun by Torquatus. He had stormed to his feet and was yelling at Fabius down upon the central dais under the golden idol of the victory. Soon the cry was repeated by those crowding the amphitheatre's tiers of benches. The very roof of the Senate house shuddered and thundered.

Torquatus slammed the butt of a staff on the ground and bellowed the challenge over and over: "Consul! Consul! Start a debate! A debate!"

What seemed to be a smaller faction tried to shout him down. Terence, seated beside me on the lowest benches where twenty of us from the legion were grouped, wearing our finest armor, leaned over to whisper:

77

"Listen! They're starting it in the streets as well. That's an ugly mob we came through—"

"I *demand* that the Carthaginian ransom be a subject for debate!" Torquatus roared. The hundreds packed in the open doorways and the porches of the *curia,* not to mention the thousands more jamming the sunlit forum, heard the cry and repeated it:

"Debate!"

*"Let there be debate!"*

"CONSUL! CONSUL!"

With a weary shrug, I said to Terence, "Don't look so surprised. We're here to speak on the matter, aren't we?"

Dismayed, the tribune fingered the sword scabbard resting against his knee. "Of course. But I'm astonished at the number of people outside. Either Torquatus has done a splendid job of convincing others of our guilt, or we *are* the criminals he says we are, and just can't see it—"

"Ridiculous, Terence. They're baying animals. A claque—rabble! They don't know a thing about battle."

"All the same, I hate to see so many of them. They could—tear us apart—well, I'm glad the dress armor was called for—and this." He slapped the scabbard again.

*"There will be silence!"*

On his feet, Quintus Fabius cracked his wand of office against the curule chair in which he sat. Nearby stood the coop of sacred chickens. Earlier, the birds had pecked away at wheat grains strewn on the coop floor. The grains left uneaten had been studied by Fabius. As a member of the College of Augurs, he was in

78

a position to say that the day was favorable for conducting the business of the Senate.

Now, however, he was perplexed. The crowd refused to quiet down. People surged back and forth in the doorways. Jeers and pointed fingers were directed at us. Fabius continued clacking his wand:

"Either we will have silence or the Praetorians will clear the doors and porches." The threat did nothing to calm those outside, but it did quiet some of the spectators on the benches. When the great gallery stilled for a moment, Fabius announced:

"Debate is hereby open on the matter of the 100,000 denarii ransom demanded by Hannibal Barca, general of Carthage, for those legionnaries captured at Cannae and held prisoner by him. Let the witnesses be introduced."

One by one the veterans of Cannae stood up, spoke and sat down again, treated courteously by Fabius but hooted at by the spectators. Some of the speakers were eloquent, others less so. But all, I thought dismally, as my turn came and Fabius pointed to me, all had the odds against them, so heavily had Torquatus packed the *curia* with persons in sympathy with his views.

"Identify yourself and come forward," Fabius instructed me.

I gave my name and ranks, both my former and present ones. As I started for the rostrum, out on the portico to my rear, someone exclaimed loudly, "Linus Julius, did he say? Why, that's—"

I didn't bother to turn around. Immediately other voices silenced the first. I mounted the three steps, I was grateful that the injunction to silence had been heeded, if only for the moment. My hands sweated as I gripped both edges of the rostrum and stared out over those venerable men in togas, many quite old. Slowly, I began to speak:

"Many false tales have been spread about Cannae. The tale that it was a trap laid by the Carthaginians may be true. But it was a clever trap. Once sprung, it nearly wiped us out to the last man."

Here I paused, swallowing hard. Varro wore an expression of relief. I don't know what he had expected from me, but I saw no reason to worsen the situation by picking at wounds already raw; Varro's bungling was public knowledge.

A bit more confident, I went on:

"The eighty who escaped, led by the honorable tribune who was first to speak from this platform, did so not merely to save their own lives—though I could never stand here and deny self-interest played no part—but to fight again for this, their mother city. We who escaped won our freedom only through a bit of luck and the blessing of the gods—"

That was a pretty fiction; it had taken determination as well. I despised the men who had not come with us out of the pens. Still, they were soldiers, and I was willing to bend the truth a little for the benefit of all who served:

"It would not be just to call the prisoners who remained behind cowards. Rather, call them men who took a different way of preserving themselves so that they, too, might once again rally to the Republic's defense." I let my voice rise. "You must all be clear about this. Every man who served at Cannae fought hard. Those who fled before the battle ended did so with one reason in mind—the reason I have noted. To return to Rome, renew their strength, and fight again. Those of us who escaped were guided by the same motive, and our wish has been fulfilled. But those still held by Hannibal, no matter how strong their desire to once more raise their swords, cannot do so without the help of this venerable group. Ransom them. Not only for the sake of their families, but more important, for the sake of our Republic—before the Carthaginian host sweeps down and there is no longer a Roman army to—"

Movement in the corner of my eye made me hesitate.

"—no Roman army to defend the walls of this city which—"

The words died in my throat as I saw a face hovering behind the shoulder of old Torquatus.

Fabius frowned, annoyed. "Continue, please! Our time is valuable."

"He has no right to continue," Torquatus rumbled, on his feet once again. "I demand Senatorial privilege. I demand the floor! I further demand that this man be removed."

"What's the meaning of this interruption," Fabius asked. "Who is that person with you?"

"A legionary who only today returned to Rome," Torquatus said. "A man who—"

"—escaped like the rest of us!" I shouted, rage and fear making me reckless. "Let him tell you what he did, he and his noble companion!"

Once more Fabius rapped for silence—from me this time. But a hush fell over the whole place. The hundreds packing the doors and porches wanted to know what the simply dressed, squat man had told Torquatas as he sought him out at his bench during my speech. The man stood very close to the graybeard, laughing at me with his mouth and one good eye. He

81

must have been the one who had cried my name a while ago—

Quinux. The raping legionary.

"Push that disgraceful excuse for a soldier off the rostrum," Torquatus exclaimed, waving at me. "Here at my side is a true soldier! That's right, Linus Julius, he won't deny it. He's a man from the field of Cannae like you, but a brave one for a change—" He turned slightly, playing to the gallery. "This good and devoted man, Quinux, saw a fellow soldier named Polidor slain by a person in this room. Who? There! That man on the rostrum who now begs and whines for money—" He flung a pointing hand at me. "Linus Julius, I accuse you of the highest crime of which a legionary can be adjudged guilty. The murder of another soldier. Quinux is the witness who will swear to it."

I started to yell an angry rebuttal. Torquatus out-shouted me:

"Is that one of your brave men, Romans? Is that one of your noble warriors who fled to fight another day? Are a thousand or ten thousand like him worth spending one Roman coin to save their cowardly hides? I say *no!*"

Pandemonium broke loose. The *curia* shook as the mob shouted back, "*No! No!*"

I pounded on the rostrum, trying to get attention. Quinux rushed up and down the nearby aisles spreading his tale as quickly as possible. I shouted over the din:

"I killed Polidor because he tried to assault a woman!"

"Cowards, murderers, traitors," the mob was chanting as its members pressed forward.

"Listen to me!" I cried. "*Listen to the truth!*"

"Cowards!"

*"Hannibal's Heroes!"*

*"Show them we know they're traitors and dogs!"*

*"Kill that one!"*

*"KILL THEM ALL!"*

Groups of men incited to hysterical pitch were fighting their way down the aisles. I could smell the sweat of the mob; hear the thunder of its coming. The spectators had become men who would kill on request; maim for a whim; die to settle a trivial grudge—

Senators were stumbling over one another, sensing all too late that Quinux had released a whirlwind. Terentius Varro staggered to his feet, appealing to Dictator Fabius:

"Who is to say what is the truth? Perhaps the soldier needed killing— I insist you ascertain the facts before you judge."

"Will you sit down, you drunken sop!" Fabius bawled. There is no time! *Praetorians!* Stop those men in the aisles! Push them back! Order! Order! I demand order"

With a thunderous crash, one of the benches from the tiers was thrown down against the foot of the dais. Fabius turned pale. The wand of office dropped from his hand and skidded along the floor. He signalled to a dozen Praetorians who sped down from the back to quickly surround him with spears and push a path for him through the packed mob.

The Cannae veterans, Terence in the forefront, gathered at the foot of the rostrum, back to back, waiting. I leaped down to join them. I was unable to believe what I saw. The mob was spilling into the *curia,* pushing back Praetorians, piling down across the benches. Hannibal would have been amused.

"Cowards!"

*"Traitors!"*

"GET THEM!"

"Pull your swords," Terence barked over his shoulder. "We'll have to fight our way clear."

One of the men protested: "Kill those people? Our fellow citizens?"

"What do you think they intend to do to us? Kiss and thank us? *Look out!*"

Into our group thudded another of the benches, knocking two men flat. I heard curses and cries of pain. By now the Praetorians assigned to keep order were melting away, for they had to control the larger crowd outside, where a far greater riot might erupt.

The mob moved slowly but steadily down toward us, pushed by the weight of numbers from behind. On the topmost tier, Quinux and Torquatus watched the melee, plainly enjoying it. Suddenly Terence pointed to a possible escape route up a less congested aisle where three spear-armed Praetorians struggled with just a handful of citizens.

In only moments, the riot had lost its political motivation and became an orgy of looting. Several senators were being stripped of their jeweled amulets, their protests lost in the general outcry. One group of looters headed for Torquatus and Quinux. The graybeard dived for a tunnel into the adjoining temple.

Quinux tried to take the same path at the same time. The old senator grew frantic; threw himself against the one-eyed soldier. Quinux toppled off the top tier, his head and body smashing against the lower tiers as he fell—

On signal from Terence, our wedge mounted the aisle. The armored backs of the Praetorians were just a short distance ahead. Beyond their spears, perhaps fifty or sixty screaming men awaited us now. But the sight of our drawn swords made them hesitate.

An unearthly scream ran out as Quinux finally struck the floor of the *curia,* bringing down a pile of benches with him. His skull hit the corner of the rostrum and popped open like a rotten fruit. I had no time to take any satisfaction. As we dodged past the Praetorians, angry men rushed at us from either side of the aisle, leaping for our throats and driven back only by our flailing swords.

Thus we fled that dreadful scene. As we passed from the high tier onto the sunlit porch and headed down into the Forum on the run, bowling aside all who got in our path, a Praetorian back at the doorway cried:

"Some of them have already gone to destroy your camp. Run—and good luck to you!"

# CHAPTER XII

# CONFRONTATION

Fights had broken out all across the Forum. Terence led us away down dark side streets. We fled on the run, our swords bared.

In neighboring thoroughfares, an angry, thunderous tide of voices could be heard. At intersections we glimpsed bands of men with staffs, rocks and other crude weapons. They were all headed in one direction—to our camp area.

From afar, we saw several thousand angry citizens streaming toward the main gates. We turned off, took a different route, and approached our own encampment by way of that of the Praetorians. Inside the stockade, absolute chaos reigned. Officers rushed up and down, ordering maniples to defense posts. The rumbling of the approaching mob filled the air. The noise was astonishing—an ocean of sound that bathed and physically stunned the senses.

As the twenty of us split apart, running for our various units, Consul Varro and a group of officers came spurring down the company street. I was ducking inside my tent for my battle armor when the consul recognized me:

"There's the man! Linus Julius!"

Fearfully I turned. Then my fear changed from concern about myself to worry about the fate of the whole encampment. Varro's eyes were glazed. Two officers reached out to prop him in the saddle as he swayed. He pointed at me with a palsied hand.

"The charge against you will be investigated at a suitable time. But for the present—"

His jowls began to shake as he listened to the mounting tumult outside the stockade. Quickly he covered his eyes. An officer seized the bridle of his horse and led it away.

A few minutes later I buckled on my armor, picked up my pilum and sprinted for my assigned post with my maniple. Already men were hammering on the barred gates:

"Kill the cowards! Break in! *Destroy everything*—!"

One of my men stopped me: "Sir, the worst news has just—"

"Nothing can be worse than this," I snapped at him. "We'll have to kill hundreds to stop them."

"Fabius is coming to take charge. Varro has retired to his tent in the center of the camp." The man glowered from under his helmet, contemptuous. "They say he began weeping. Weeping and shuddering and calling for wine."

So we were without even a commander worthy of the name. Fabius would surely not arrive in time.

"*Form ranks, there!*" I shouted, pushing my men into the three-row defense formation in the center of the street which paralleled the outer wall. We crouched down, sweating in our armor; waiting. A sub-centurion ran up to inform me that someone with an urgent message was looking for me in the adjoining street.

"—and you'd better get him out of here before this breaks," my informant finished. "He's hardly ten years old. He's been hanging around for hours, waiting for your return."

Turning cold, I started away. "Hold my place, Tyrrhus. You're in command until I come back."

Long before I reached him, I recognized the pinch-faced sweeping boy from the tavern. He looked alternately excited and fearful at having been caught in the center of so much noise, so much danger.

"I came at sunup," the boy explained. "I didn't know you would be in the Forum, sir. Last night a nobleman's bearers with a closed chair called for the lady. She hasn't returned."

"Where did she go? Quick lad, speak!"

"A *domus* on the Via Repentia. The great *domus* of the Pulvian *gens*."

"The *Pulvian?*" The name seemed to burn on my tongue. Then an evil suspicion began to form. At first, I thought it impossible. Then I recalled the handsome, twisted face in the saddle at Cannae; the stiff, ruined leg—

The monster who had waited for the right chance.

I shook the boy. "Are you absolutely certain it was the *domus* of the Pulvius family?"

He wrenched away, alarmed. "Certain! I asked a

vendor. It's barred and shuttered, and no one came out after the lady was admitted."

"Can you show me the way?"

He goggled. "Of course, master. But isn't your place here?"

"My place is in that damn house, finding out what's happened to her. Run, boy—run fast or I'll split you open like a Carthaginian!"

The Via Repentia curved around the summit of the Esquiline hill, lined on both sides with one magnificent *domus* after another. Clouds moved across the sun, bathing the cobbled ways in a shifting, uncertain light. All at once, with an instinct for danger probably bred in him since birth, the tavern boy stopped and pointed.

"It is the second *domus* on the right. I go no further, master. I have earned my pay."

Truly he had. Fear shone in his fox eyes; he knew a deserted street in a fine neighborhood must hold some special horror to make me desert the camp in time of crisis. I started away.

"Will they kill you in there, master?"

I halted, uncertain. "No, it's the girl's life I'm fearful about. I thank you for what you've done. Good-bye."

"Good-bye, master. Thank you for the coins."

He turned and sped away down the hill. Drawing my cloak around me, I proceeded along the street as though I were a soldier bent upon some official miision. When I was sure of not being observed, I darted into a passage between the great houses and emerged shortly in a sour alley at the rear of the *domus*.

The rustling in the shrubbery ought to have warned me. *"Fall on him!"* Slaves crashed through the hedge.

90

Up came my sword, a mite too late. For this was no chance discovery but a clear trap. There were a dozen of them, big men with ear hoops of gold, and coarse, swarthy faces. There are times only a fool resists; times when struggle can only bring mutilation. Death. No gain. I let two of the men seize my arms. Another nearly broke my wrist taking the sword. A third whipped a dagger out of his girdle and pricked the flesh of my neck:

"Shall we carry you to the lord of the house alive, soldier? He would be angry if we were forced to bring you to him dead. It is up to you."

"How is it you were waiting for me?" I said.

They laughed and pushed me toward the kitchen entrance. The leader said, "Do you think we missed the boy trailing after the litter when it came from the inn last night? After all, it's our duty to keep an eye peeled for thieves. We caught the lad and frightened him some. Then we paid him to make sure you learned what we *wanted* you to learn. Our welcome was easy to arrange. The master assured us that you would not try the atrium doors, like a regular caller. The only other way in is that garden wall you climbed. Move along!"

A knee in the spine pitched me forward into the steaming kitchen. They rushed me unceremoniously to the peristyle. So the tavern boy had taken double payment to insure my betrayal! Perhaps that was why he'd asked if they would kill me. For a moment—but only a moment—conscience had gotten the better of him.

"Master, you have a visitor!" the chief slave crowed.

They dropped me like a bag of grain on a marble bench in the center of the peristyle.

The peristyle's sky draperies were furled back so

91

sunlight could shine down. The man on the nearby bench was seated comfortably, left leg thrust out beneath the toga with its narrow purple stripe. He looked far cleaner and healthier than when I'd last seen him in battlefield armor. His black hair was in ringlets, faintly perfumed. Gems glittered on his fingers. Yet the eyes were the same as at Cannae. They were black, and full of long-remembered hatred.

"You've done well, Sardyz," he said. "Withdraw now, but only to the passage. Keep your knives handy. Being a soldier, this lout might be rash enough to lay hands on me. Though of course that would do him little good. And less good for the person in whom he's interested."

So saying, Sardus Pulvius waved. Jewels on his fingers flashed. The slaves withdrew.

"Where is she?" I said. "Dead already?"

Pulvius chuckled. "What a crude, common fellow you are! Kill her? Not I. And if you had any wits, you'd have detected this little deception, hey?"

He poured wine from an amphora into a silver cup. His eyes glittered above the rim as he drank. "But then you never suspected the man who first located you, either. Actually, I had a score of such low types combing Rome. The one who found you kept watch on you and received an extra-fat purse. He did mention you chased him one night—"

Memory swept back, bringing to mind the horse-toothed fellow in the clothes of a carter; the one I had pursued from the inn of Castor and Pollux, assuming—wrongly—that he was an armor thief.

Pulvius continued to sip his wine, drawing out the confrontation as long as possible.

"Let's get it done," I said, climbing to my feet. "Set

your butchers on me and I'll take some of them with me when I go."

He smiled an exquisite smile. "Oh, my dear man! Do you think I'd resort to such crudities? After all, I have been searching for you ever since I returned to the city. Once my agent who discovered you at the military camp followed you to that little inn and learned you had somehow connected yourself with a woman—a charming woman, I might add—all thought of killing you left my mind."

Slowly Pulvius heaved himself to his feet. He hitched toward me, the stiff leg in its leather sandal dragging a path in the grass.

"At first, when I lost you at Cannae—for how could I kill you before Varro himself?—nothing seemed more important than one day watching you die. The presence of the woman in your life caused me to revise my plans."

Although I was sorely afraid, I tried not to show it. I stood still, and even managed a rude laugh. "What a splendid person you are! A coward who ran away. A secret man afraid of daylight."

The brief flare in his eyes told me I had wounded his pride. He remained composed, however, leaning over to inhale the fragrance of a blossoming bush.

"Then you guessed that I never returned to the army following Cannae. You're perfectly right. I had a horse under me, my life intact. I choose to call what I did prudence, not cowardice." Pulvius straightened up. "Unlike a *common soldier*—"

"Common," I broke in. "Again and again you use that word—"

"Yes! Because you are! Common as dirt. A lump of clay."

"That stiff leg says otherwise. It says I was a better rider than you. It reminds you—always. Gods, what a sick creature you must be to nurse a hatred for such a long time—"

*"Silence!"* He flung the wine cup's contents all in my face.

The outburst brought the slaves rushing to his aid. He shuddered, covered his face with his hands a moment, then waved them back. Leaning down, he picked up the empty goblet. The mocking smile returned to his mouth.

"That was a point scored for you," he said, barely whispering. "If you saw me with my guard down for a moment, that victory is a small one. For after this meeting, I will continue to live as I always have. While you—"

He shrugged. "You will not live at all."

It was foolish of me to try to provoke his anger. Yet I could not stand still and await his pleasure like some sacrificial ox. Perhaps the hopelessness of the trap lent me a little courage, too. I had nothing to lose—

"What do you intend to do?" I asked. "Remain in this house all your life, a cowering cripple who ran away? May the gods pity you, nobleman."

His composure remained unshaken by that. He shrugged. "Of course I shan't remain here." He started to stroll around the peristyle as though he were a pedant explaining a favorite subject. "I merely chose to travel by myself from Cannae to Rome because I did not care to risk public scorn by rejoining the forces left to that idiot Varro. As it turned out, I judged the situation accurately—the situation, and the reaction of certain segments of the Roman populace as well. What is it they're calling you——?" He tittered. "Oh, yes. Hannibal's Heroes."

He relished the amusement a moment, then went on, "That is a distinction I can do without. I entered Rome quietly, by night, and I intend to remain in this *domus* until the hue and cry have died down. No one outside will discover who's in this house. Money silences plain inquisitive tradespeople. When the stigma of having served at Cannae has been forgotten, I shall reappear, having wandered through Latium, wounded and out of my senses for months—some pretty story of that sort will serve to explain my absence. They'll welcome me back with open arms!"

Abruptly his head lifted, cocked to one side. A pounding had started at the atrium gates. In the distance I heard a flurry of footfalls. Within moments, the chief slave rushed in again.

Pulvius frowned at the interruption. The slave bent close, whispering. I watched Pulvius's face change from peevishness to delight. Then he nodded briskly:

"Excellent tidings! Better than I'd hoped for. Pay the man well for his patience in waiting for the announcement. Then bring in the little whore."

The word flayed my temper like a whip. I took a step toward him but his raised hand held me back:

"Don't, Linus Julius. Not unless you wish me to give an order for them to hurt her."

The sun drowned behind flying clouds. All the peristyle was in shadow when three of the slaves appeared with Nara.

# CHAPTER XIII

# *SOLDIER'S FATE*

As the slaves retreated, she tried to accustom her eyes to the change of light. Her hair was in wild disarray, and she looked dazed.

The *palla* she wore, though it was fine red wool, was ripped in many places. Through a tear above her right breast I saw a livid yellow bruise.

Slowly her head swung around to Pulvius—then to me.

"Come, my dear," he said politely. "Greet our unannounced guest."

Recognition lit her eyes. *"Julius!"* she began crying.

She ran toward me. With his outstretched hand Pulvius caught her and jerked her around so hard, she moaned.

"No, my dear. I can't allow him to touch you. I prefer to have your high-minded savior look at you and wonder what I did with you all last night."

"That's plain enough, isn't it?" Savagely, she tore down the shoulder of the *palla*. The right breast was exposed, patchy with several bruise-marks. A molten lump formed in my throat as I watched her try to accuse Pulvius with her body.

True to his nature, he could not be moved. His wave was casual, almost cheerful as he dismissed her. To me he said:

"The poor child got rather hysterical with me, Julius. What did she expect when she hired herself out to my steward? Easy caresses? Mouthings of poetry? Respect? For a *gutter girl?*" He tittered again.

"Julius warned me," Nara breathed. "He tried to tell me of the perversions—" She began sobbing, shaking her head from side to side. "The things—the shameful things you did—"

She couldn't go on.

Pulvius smiled. "I did none of them for your benefit, my dear. Or in truth, for mine either. Rather, for his."

"What kind of game is this?" I demanded. "Am I supposed to whine for your mercy? Your forbearance? I won't. Because I know I won't get it—and because I feel the same toward you as you do toward me."

Born to the nobility, he was trained never to show his inner feelings except under the firmest kind of control. But that control was slipping again. He managed to regain it; tented his fingers thoughtfully and returned to his seat on the bench. All the while I was conscious of the pack of servants lurking somewhere behind. Despite the threat they presented, I was afraid my reason and my caution would crumble any moment—

Pulvius said, "All I expect you to do, Julius, my

98

friend, is to make a simple choice—you and your gutter girl between you. In a few minutes one of you will be free to leave this *domus*. As for the other, that one will remain." His eyes burned with sudden amusement:

"And will be disposed of in due time. However, I leave entirely to your choice the matter of who goes free and who enjoys my continued hospitality."

Like a captive turned on a rack I felt my nerves crying out, *kill him!* The trap was all the more damnable because, once free, one of us would be forever haunted by the death of the other. In truth, there was no real choice.

As Nara stared at him, trying to comprehend, I said, "Release her. I will remain your prisoner."

He didn't like that. Nor could he mask his distaste, no matter how hard he tried. The control of a patrician apparently had its limits.

"Surely she has some say in the matter!" he exclaimed. "What are your wishes, my dear?"

"Julius—" she tried to reach me with her eyes across a widening gulf of horror and fright. "What you said about the appetites of the fine men of Rome—" Memories gagged her, forcing her knuckles to her mouth.

Like a patron at an amusing theatrical spectacle, Pulvius helped himself to more wine from the amphora. I hardly saw. Nothing existed except Nara's bleak gaze trying to reach the root of my soul and say what her dry, abused mouth could only say haltingly:

"I was so wrong and foolish to sell myself. I—I never really dreamed men like this existed. I never knew there are men who harbor such vileness—such hate—"

Again she ran to me. This time he permitted it. She beat her fists against my arms:

"Go free! Go free while this accursed man is agreeable to it—!"

"Stand back." His voice was raised very slightly. "Stand back or I'll call for a lash."

But Nara would not be cowed: "Julius, go—I beg you!" Tears sprang forth then, nearly breaking my heart.

"I love you, Julius. I haven't known it till this moment—"

"Then it's decided," Pulvius declared, his lips pursing; he was pleased. He clapped once, loudly. "Return the girl to her quarters!"

"Nothing's decided!" I shouted. "If you hate me so much, why do you want her here?"

"I have my reasons, soldier. You'll soon forget this little tart—"

The slaves rushed forward, swarming around Nara, pulling her away. Some vast and evil force swirled near us, beyond my comprehension. *I* was the one he despised, and I could not conceive of him taking more pleasure from killing her slowly than from killing me in the same way. Perhaps he was wholly insane, yet I doubted that.

I dug my nails in my palms. "Once more, Pulvius—*I* am the one you want. I am the one to stay."

He shook his head, smiling that cursed little smile. "No."

One of the slaves manhandling Nara whispered something filthy and put his hand over her bare nipple. She recoiled, clawing at him. The man slapped her. The clouds passed from the sun. Pulvius's face leaped out bright and reason died within me.

I charged him like a deranged man, closing my hands around his throat; strangling and strangling, mindlessly—

"Get him off! Pull him off!" he shrieked.

His eyes bulged like currants. My hands tightened. His tongue popped out of his mouth. Then, from behind, a cudgel crashed against my head. My fingers slipped. Half a dozen of the slaves dragged me away from him—

They beat me with their thick staffs. I swung at them, to maim and kill. One reeled back with his left eye torn out, a bleeding hole. Then the great brute who led the slaves swung his cudgel at my temple. The whole world exploded.

I tumbled to my knees, retching. Another blow struck the back of my neck. Surely they would kill me now. Surely this was the end. I had failed—

Pulvius was rubbing his throat. But he was smiling. His body seemed to grow and distort, looming against the blue heavens above the peristyle. As the scene began to spin, I had a last glimpse of Nara, tears streaming down her face—

Then I saw nothing.

When I wakened, I thought that I had descended into hell.

I lay in some sort of muck-slimed ditch. Smoke blew through the darkness all around me. My body ached. Yet it still seemed a real, solid body.

I staggered upright, blinking and choking. Some of the smoke drifted away. I saw smashed log walls; tents flapping in the wind. Far off in the murk a silver eagle gleamed in torchlight.

Slowly I grew aware of sounds: horses pulling heavy

wagons; soldiers barking orders—the whole confusion of a military camp that had been ravaged. For some unknown reason, Pulvius's men had dumped me into a latrine ditch outside the ruins of what had once been the camp of the Cannae veterans.

Nowhere in the darkness did I see a sign of the mob, only legionary armor. Like one drugged, I walked through the demolished gates. Two citizens lay dead just inside. Their bellies had been ripped open with swords. One still clutched a stone in his lifeless hand.

I stopped a centurion directing a carpenter's wagon. "What happened? There is so much destruction—"

"Move along and find your unit! They must have knocked you out of action early, or else you'd know."

"Know what?"

*"Get that wagon out of here! Keep this street open!"*

The vehicle went lurching away between the smouldering ashes of tents put to the torch. The centurion turned, wiping sweat from his face.

"We lost twenty or so. But those fools in the mob lost a hundred or more before the Praetorians arrived to help us stop the riot. I wish they'd run a blade through my guts, too. We fight for them and they turn on us and send us to exile—look, I can't stand here talking. I'm responsible for this gate, and for seeing that no soldier tries to escape. Even though I have half a mind to go myself."

"What did you say about exile?" I asked. "Tell me! I belong to this legion just as you do—"

"Your bad luck," he said with a sad shrug. "After the riot in the *curia,* the Senate reconvened. They voted against ransoming the prisoners. The ten hostages have already been sent back to Hannibal. When Fabius rode in with the Praetorians to take com-

102

mand, he quelled the riot by issuing his proclamation. That's all that stopped the citizens from tearing us to pieces—the decree of Fabius. Issued to renew the public morale!"

And he gathered spit in his mouth and blew it on the ground, shaking.

"Where—where are they sending us? Tell me that much more."

I had seldom seen such pain in a man's eyes; perhaps they looked as grieving as my own.

"Sicily."

"*Sicily!* The end of the earth—!"

"Not quite. But a close substitute. Two legions are going, under that sot Varro." One by one he ticked off the horrors on his fingers. "We are to receive no pay. We are forbidden to build winter quarters within a day's march of any town. We are to remain in exile as long as the war against the Carthaginians lasts. Fabius said he had no choice. He maintained the Senate would have overthrown him if he didn't take some step to pacify the people—"

His laugh was ragged. "So you see, we really are a traitor's army now. 'Hannibal's Heroes.' "

I turned, disbelieving, and stumbled up the street of smouldering tents. As I walked, the truth of it descended on me. No longer did I wonder about the whispered news Pulvius had received in the peristyle. He had planned the best of all punishments for each of his captives. He had wanted Nara to remain so that I could go free. Not merely alive and remembering my fate, but forever branded a traitor among other traitors—

She had lost her life, and I had lost the only real possession a soldier carries with him throughout his days—his honor. Some of it had been stolen at Cannae, the rest when my quarrel with Pulvius had led her to her death. Only a man who had known how kind Nara could be, and who had also known campaigning would understand why I would gladly have changed places with her.

Three days later, a fleet of galleys loaded at the Tiber port of Ostia. They weighed anchor and bore out across the blue sea, carrying Hannibal's Heroes—

Every damned one of us.

## Part Two

# THE EAGLES IN EXILE

# CHAPTER I

# A PRIVATE QUARREL

"Swallow the words, Rufio!" came the jeer. "Else Julius will force you."

"Yes," I said, peeling off my tunic and taking a better grip on the pilum. "This moment, my loudmouthed friend."

Rufio was thick-chested, lump-nosed and arrogant. He spat at me, then tossed his spear into the air and caught it with one powerful hand. "Greek!" he said contemptuously. Several of the legionnaires in a hastily formed ring snickered. "I will prove what I said by ramming this iron down your throat. You've grown as soft as a lovebird."

"Someone keep watch for the tribune," a soldier yelled. "This may go the route."

Once more I repeated it: "Yes. There is one thing to

do with this human dung heap and that's to punish him."

"Try, Greek," Rufio laughed, crouching with his spear held point forward, at the ready.

We were both stripped to the waist. We circled one another, gauging each other's reach. Behind Rufio rose the bleak pattern of Sicily's wild, lonely mountains. All around the drill field, maniples were running through a listless catapult exercise, as mine had been doing before Rufio fancied I had stumbled against him and caused him to spoil a shot.

Rufio and I had quarreled before. He was a man naturally inclined to quarrelling. This time, to judge from his expression, we were going to settle our differences once and for all time.

With a quick thrust of the spear, he pierced my shoulder. As he danced back I lunged for his belly. And missed.

"What's the matter, Greek? All the nights of lovesick mooning have made you slow, hey?"

Abruptly he lowered his shoulders and streaked across the circle with speed surprising in a man so heavy. His spear flashed down at my sandaled foot. I jumped out of the way. He pivoted as he rushed by, cursing. I jabbed and sliced through the bunched muscle of his bared forearm. He paled but didn't hesitate. He came forward.

His arm was a red fountain. He drove his pilum at my belly. I hacked down from overhead. At the last instant he darted aside. Instead of hitting me, he bowled into me with his shoulder. I crashed on my back with the wind knocked out of me.

"Unfair, unfair, the pilum only!" someone cried.

As we trotted to the catapults to resume our drill, Rufio took the opportunity to bait me again. As he rubbed his throat, he smiled, indicating that fortune had in turn smiled upon him, saving him today so that we could encounter each other in the future. Dismally I knew that he was probably right. Men without women grow into savages.

In military terms, we were little better than boys playing at war. Stationed in the hills above the island's eastern shore, payless and never allowed near a village, we felt not only humiliation keenly but futility. We marched and counter-marched on lonely roads going nowhere; even the cavalrymen like me were now reduced to foot rank. Once or twice there were skirmishes with the Greek garrison from the town of Lentini, or those from the great port of Syracuse protected behind its mammoth walls, but the fights were brief and decidedly minor.

Syracuse had three distinct quarters, cities within fortified cities, which made assault almost impossible. It was still a vital harbor. Possession of it would guarantee an open supply for Hannibal in Latium. Ships ran up the middle sea from Carthage, reprovisioned at Syracuse and then slipped through the strait to rendezvous with the Thunderbolt somewhere on the Roman coast.

Nor had we any friends in Syracuse. The former tyrant, Hiero II, had been an ally of the Republic. Once he had sent tribute in the form of grain and a huge golden victory statue to the Senate. But that had happened a long time ago, at the start of the Punic war. Now Hiero II was many months dead. Since his death, according to a handful of Varro's spies, Carthaginian agents had infiltrated Syracuse. And just two months earlier, Hieronymus, who was the dead Hiero's grandson and hardly more than a boy, had declared his support of Carthage. As ruler of Syracuse, Hieronymus had dropped a fat plum into Hannibal's fingers.

Our two legions had insufficient siege equipment to reduce the port's mighty walls. Under the supervision of a praetor named Appius, several new galleys had just unloaded fresh contingents of men upon the eastern beach, however. Perhaps a new assault was being planned.

That night, over a cup of wine, I discussed this new situation with Terence, asking "Have you heard any further news?"

"As a matter of fact I have. The Senate is sending Claudius Marcellus to take charge."

"The general who marched the debtor and slave legions into the field before we sailed?"

"That very one. Apparently he defeated Hannibal in a major battle. At any rate, they've honored him by giving him the title 'The Sword of Rome' and are sending him out here to crush Syracuse."

"Do you suppose there's a chance he'd take these two legions under his standard?"

"Scant hope of it, Julius. We are still in disgrace." Across the campfire, Terence's eyes grew somber. "Let me change the subject a moment. I heard about your spear duel with Rufio."

"Well, I suppose there is no hiding the reason for it, either." I hesitated. "He said that you and I are Greek lovers."

Never have I seen Terence smile in quite such a cynical fashion. "I suspected as much. It's a common enough failing when soldiers are cooped up. I see cases of it every day and so do you. It disgusts me, men mooning around after men. Having your name dragged in the mud by scum like Rufio is a fine price to pay for friendship, isn't it? Watch out for him, Julius."

In succeeding days Terence grew increasingly gloomy, I noticed. He seemed to brood over Rufio's slurs. When I and three others appeared on the roster, ordered out on patrol duty to watch the twisting highland road running up from Syracuse to the garrison town of Lentini, I was glad to be able to get away from the place—and the snickering men—causing his depression. Terence alone, with his counsel and patience, had pulled me out of despair after we left Rome. Terence alone had lent me the strength to endure our exile, if not to relish it.

Our patrol assignment spanned three days. On the second, a noisy thunderstorm broke at dawn. Near midday I was crouching on a flat rock above the road, shivering in the scant protection of an outcrop, when I heard a lesser kind of thunder from the direction of the garrison town of Lentini.

As I stood up, a bolt of lightning illuminated a Greek chariot coming fast. Its two milky horses plunged along, wide-eyed. There seemed to be no charioteer. The vehicle swayed back and forth, bouncing dangerously.

Directly below my outpost, the road made a sharp turn. When the chariot flashed by underneath, I glimpsed a human form huddled on the floor of the car. Then the chariot's rear wheel struck a rock. The axle split. There was a tremendous crash, and the traces separated.

The person in the car was hurled out as the detached chariot tumbled down the hill below the road. The horses raced away into the rainstorm.

113

Thunder boomed as I scrambled over treacherous rocks, crossed the road, and climbed downward again. The Greek from the chariot was trying to rise on hands and knees, and having difficulty.

"Here!" I called. "Wait a moment—I'll give you a hand."

For a moment I'd forgotten I was a Roman soldier and that the chariot driver was, and must be, an enemy. Just as I remembered that I had better be wary of him, the unlucky driver turned over and stared at me.

The chariot driver was no driver at all, but a comely young woman with high-piled black hair, violet eyes, and a full fine form beneath a thin, rich gown of ivory silk.

# CHAPTER II

# THE GREEK WOMAN

Gaping, I held out a hand to assist her. She took it. As she rose, seeming more shaken than hurt, she recognized my armor.

"You're a Roman! Let me go. I need no help from your kind—!"

At that, she began to struggle. The fold of her outer cloak concealing her right arm fell aside. I saw a long, deep gash some sharp rock had put into her flesh as she tumbled. Then I noticed tiny spatters of blood on the gown. For the first time, she noticed too.

"I didn't realize I was cut—" she began. She shook her head. "Everything happened so quickly—"

"If you can bring yourself to forget I'm a Roman," I said, "I'll tear off a piece of my cloak and tie up that gash."

My use of tradesman's Greek seemed to reassure

her, although her violet eyes still showed suspicion. For further proof that I was no ravening beast, I ripped the cloth from the end of my *sagum* and held it out to her. I was so thoroughly sick of my place in the exiled legions that I was furious at the nervous look of her eyes. Those eyes said all Romans were savages—which of course included me.

"Tie it yourself, if you think I'm bent on rape!" I exclaimed.

She took the wool. Her movements grew more controlled; even a trifle haughty as she wrapped her arm and fixed a knot. Secluded as we were by the overhanging branches of a great tree, isolated a little from the full rage of the storm, I found myself again paying attention to the lovely violet hue of her eyes, and ignoring the accusing glint in them.

"You're from the fortifications back in the hills," she said.

"Quite correct. My name is Linus Julius. But since I am a Roman, and the very fact seems to offend you, I'll take my leave." I pulled my cloak around my shoulders.

"No, please—I apologize. I must thank you properly. Our people may be at war, but we needn't be. Not at this moment, anyway—"

Something made me smile. "All right. A moment's truce. The other men in my patrol will be missing me soon, though. Just let me satisfy my curiosity before I go. Why is a woman of obvious high station driving a chariot alone on this wretched road?"

"I had a driver." She gestured into the downpour. "I was traveling back from Lentini where I've been visiting kinsmen. The flash storm took us by surprise. First the chariot team bolted, then my driver was thrown off and the horses went out of control." She smiled rather pertly. "Does that answer everything?"

I had no chance to reply. A shout of, "Ho, Julius! *Where have you got to?*" drifted down.

"The other men," I explained. "I must take my leave. I assume you have a retinue?"

"Somewhere behind me on the road, yes. They should be along soon."

"Then I'll depart. I'm not under orders to fight skirmishes with slaves. Good day."

And I darted back up the hillside to intercept the three men climbing down over the rocks. For some reason I couldn't explain, I kept seeing the momentary glow of the violet eyes as she tried to thank me across the gulf of our enforced enmity.

I met the men on the road and pushed them toward the hills again:

"There'll be a party of Greek slaves along soon any moment—never mind how I know. Get out of sight so that we aren't required to use our swords on a bunch of eunuchs and women who—"

In midsentence I swung around. Lightning burst, shining on three chariots bearing down upon us. Already a faint cry of, "Romans! Roman soldiers!" carried in the beating rain.

The lady's eunuchs, a dozen strong, poured out of the braking chariots. The slaves carried short Greek swords and slings.

"Let's run for it!" I shouted to my companions. "We have no quarrel with them."

"Perhaps you don't, Julius," big yellow-headed Maximo said, throwing back his cloak. "I've been waiting for months to slip iron into some Greek guts."

117

Before I could order him to stop, he had darted up the road. The three of us remaining had no choice but to go after him, pulling our swords as we ran.

By the time we arrived, Maximo was cornered by three of the eunuchs. More were dashing to help. Maximo was far more confident than was justified:

There is a legend among full men that the half-man will not fight. This legend says the half-man, confronted by any weapon whatever, will always turn and run—and will usually be squealing as he does. So much for conventional wisdom! I had met half-men who spoke in deep voices, and whose manner showed none of the affectations frequently expected of those with their disability. I had done battle with just such half-men, and could testify that it was perilous to take them lightly. Again I saw one of the eunuchs stab mightily at Maximo's unprotected back.

I cut him down before his blade landed. The force of my blow took his head half off.

The eunuchs shrieked curses in Greek but they were not physical weaklings. A sword clanged off my breastplate. Another missed my cheek by a hair. My comrades fared less well. Two had already fallen under the weight of sheer numbers and were floundering in the mud.

"Behind you, Lucius!" I shouted to the one man still standing, even as I fended off two more eunuchs pressing in from my left. I ran one through the gut. The other whacked the side of my skull with the flat of his blade. Seconds later they had dragged me up out of the mud, disarmed.

Maximo, Lucas, and Polybix were likewise struggling and held captive. A number of slave girls had appeared from the chariots. The violet-eyed lady came hurrying from the other direction. Polybix began to weep, fearing instant death. His fear was well grounded. The chief eunuch, a greasy sort with rain dribbling down his forehead, spoke:

"May we slay them outright, Lady Cynthia, and carry their heads back to Syracuse?"

Instantly, Lady Cynthia replied, "No, I forbid it. The soldier in the center came to my aid."

"They are enemies!" the eunuch protested. "We mustn't turn them loose—"

"Turn the wiry one loose with me for a while—I'll tame him," said a different voice. One of the slave girls, a red-haired, hot-eyed wench with saucy breasts was staring at me.

The girl's remark likewise angered the lady: "Hush your tongue, Daphne!" The slave girl lowered her eyes, flushing. Lady Cynthia went on, "Baltho, I understand and would normally approve of your zealousness in regard to our enemies. On the other hand, as I mentioned, this particular soldier showed me a kindness when my chariot overturned. I will not have him harmed by our hands. Lentini is much closer than Syracuse—we'll carry all of them to the commandant there." She looked almost regretful as she added, "Turn the chariots around."

As she passed me, her glance seemed to warn that her eunuchs were fanatical men, and would possibly mutiny if she tried to free us. In turning us to Lentini, I suppose she thought she was choosing the least dangerous alternative.

Grumbling, the eunuchs hustled us to another chariot. Once more I caught the little red-haired slave girl, Daphne, watching me. In that dismal rain and in that grim situation, her twisting hips and lewd glances left me totally unmoved.

We jounced up the road to the garrison town. Maximo, his hands lashed behind his back like mine, said: "A wonderful fix! We owe it all to you, Julius—you and your kindly instincts."

"At least we're alive. That's more than we would be if we'd fought this pack of yipping dogs. Be thankful for small blessings. We'll find a way out."

The prophecy seemed foolish by the time we were taken to the Greek headquarters and thrown into a stone-ceilinged dungeon which looked out at ground level on a muddy courtyard. Of the Lady Cynthia I had seen nothing since our arrival.

About an hour later, guards fetched me out. I was taken to a chamber where a swart, well-dressed young Greek with red-veined eyes strutted round and round me, inspecting me as if I were so much meat on a hook.

"So this is the might of Rome, hey?" Pausing in front of me, he slapped me full in the face.

I lunged at him. The soldiers holding my arms pulled me back. The reason for the young man's high rage soon became apparent:

"Let me introduce myself. I am Kyron, second in command to Lord Hippocrates, who is the leader of the Greek armies of Syracuse. The Lady Cynthia has been making inquiries about you, soldier. She wants to know whether something can be done to mitigate your punishment as a prisoner. Since I am temporarily in charge here, it would be on my say-so."

He leaned close, smiling unpleasantly. "However, I have quite a personal interest in the lady's welfare. I rather resent her concern over a commoner—and a

Roman to boot. The lady's a widow, you see. Her husband was a wealthy merchant in Syracuse. She is also the half sister of Hippocrates, whom I mentioned."

I was aghast that I'd fallen in with a relative of the worst enemy we Romans had on the entire island. Yet that was of lesser concern than the immediate danger—this preening pigeon's jealousy of anyone else the lady noticed. Almost as though he couldn't restrain himself, Kyron struck me again.

"Why she would even lower herself to acknowledge the likes of you, I'll never know. I did hint I'd do something to alter your fate. So I shall. Instead of a quick death, I think we'll arrange for you and your comrades to enjoy one that's slow. Excruciatingly slow—guards! Get him out of here before I kill him myself!"

The last thing I saw before the chamber door shut was Kyron's sulking yet oddly triumphant face.

# CHAPTER III

# THE GROVE OF LOVE

It was at sundown the following day when the guards came for young Polybix. Kicking and fighting, Lucius went out the next night. The night after that, they took Maximo. My spirits fell so low, I might have killed myself on the fourth day except that the bare cell offered no means to do so.

Late in the afternoon the cell door squeaked back unexpectedly. Dim sunlight slanted into the cell. To my surprise, I saw, instead of the soldier, a wrinkled, yellow-skinned old Greek who tossed me a bundle.

"Take this. Put it on. Hurry down the corridor on the left and out. Climb into the vegetable cart you'll find drawn up, burrow underneath, and say nothing until the cart comes to a stop."

Was this some trap of Kyron's? Possibly, but I decided to risk it in order to get out of that wretched cell.

I slipped into the cloak. At a bend in the corridor, I glimpsed a Greek soldier watching me and the old man. The soldier glanced away in guilty fashion. He had the look of the bribed if ever I'd seen it.

I ran then; filled with hope at long last, I ran.

The cart was in place outside. No driver was visible, nor anyone else. Within moments I had buried myself under a load of gamy-smelling cabbages. Suddenly the cart jerked forward.

I rode that way for what seemed an hour or more. Then the cart halted. Cabbages tumbled away. The man from the prison was pulling them off me.

"I can't afford to be seen on this road," he whispered. "We must make haste. Get up the hill and into that grove and you'll find your benefactor. Though why she'd help a Roman is beyond me." He scuttled to the cart seat and was soon lashing his mules down the Lentini road which here wound through wild, straggling foothills.

I ran to the grove of ash trees he had pointed out. Deep within the grove, a random beam of sun gleamed on a brazen chariot wheel. The swollen sun was sinking, casting reddish light over the countryside. A shadow-shape stirred among the trees. A moment later the Lady Cynthia stood before me, muffled up in a cloak.

Her first words were simple and sorrowful:

"I was not in time for the others. I tried. But the bribery of soldiers is a slow process sometimes."

"And a perilous one. I thank you. Perhaps my three comrades do too, wherever they are. I hope they know I'm alive to repay that butcher Kyron one day."

A heartsick light shone in her eyes. "Yes, he's an animal. It's all the worse because he fancies I might care for him—" She shook her head. "The stupid vanity of men!"

"Tell me why you came to my aid," I said. "Solely because I helped you?"

"Partly, of course. But partly because I think my sympathy lies with Rome rather than Carthage. Not that I conceive of your Senate as any great bargain as a ruling body, mind you. But I do know my father's son by his first wife—my half-brother Hippocrates—all too well."

"I have heard the name Hippocrates," I told her. "Kyron mentioned it."

"Have you heard how he pretends to be the friend of the people of Syracuse, their defender and champion, only to promote his own cause? He'd like to assume full power. Had you heard that too?"

I shook my head.

"Well, I'm sure of it. He's a cold, ambitious, scheming man. Never to be trusted for one instant! I'm sure he's only waiting for the proper moment to remove the young tyrant, Hieronymus, who isn't much of a ruler but is at least honest and decent. Above everything, Hippocrates has ambition to be the overlord of Syracuse."

"And you? Would you really prefer Roman rule to that of your half-brother?"

"If it came to such a test of loyalty, yes."

I walked over and after a moment's hesitation touched her shoulder. "Politics aside, Lady Cynthia, I owe you a great debt of gratitude for your help."

She put her cool palm on my hand where it lay on her shoulder. Then she drew back, flushed. Her voice was low against the whisper of the ashwood leaves:

"Forgive my boldness. Now and again I forget the

station that became my lot when I married my husband."

"Kyron informed me that you were widowed—"

"Going on four years now. A long time." Violet lights in her eyes were burning brightly. Without knowing exactly why, I reached for her and planted a quick kiss on her mouth. She drew back again, more from propriety than anger, I thought.

"That was forward of you. Gratitude?"

"To use your word—partly. Also because you are an exceedingly beautiful woman."

Again she hesitated. "Then I did not mind it. Nor would I again."

On the lips of some, it would have been a whore's enticement. Upon hers it was a soft statement springing from the loneliness of the grove, from her widowhood and her own independent turn of mind, which clearly did not mirror that of her people. She was an enemy; highborn. But I had gone too long without the feel of a woman's mouth against mine. I pulled her to me a trifle roughly—

At first her kiss was gentle; almost chaste. Then her lips began to heat. Her cloak fell back. I lay a hand on her breast. For an hour in the midst of war, we forgot war and knew each other.

She was modest. Yet having been a wife gave her a certain fire, as when I touched her nude body after her gown and girdles had been dropped away. She trembled and pressed her mouth on my bare arm.

Again I kissed her, feeling her lips part. Her breath flamed against my chest when we lay together in the glow of the sunset. Trumpets and halloos and hoofbeats sounded on the roadway now. Searchers. It did not matter. Nothing mattered except the sweet warmth

126

of her flanks bending beneath mine. She moaned softly, then wildly, out of some deep need—

Those moments, as always, were the same and yet as different as ever. Only a few motions are both possible and pleasurable, and they are motions a man will have performed hundreds and hundreds of times with as many women as the gods permit him to know. In some strange way, however, it is always different as well. And with her it was especially sweet—

What lent that moment its particular savor? Perhaps it was the fact that I'd escaped death. Perhaps it was the scent with which she anointed herself. Or perhaps the way her hair fell, and her breasts rose, and her body surged forward and back and forward again. It was a joyous mystery I would never solve. Nor did I try too hard.

What I did was take the woman again. And yet again.

Presently the stars shone. We sat in the grove, talking about ourselves; our lives until this moment. At last she said:

"The hour is late, Julius. For me to stay out of Lentini any longer would cause suspicion."

"Then go." It seemed the hardest thing I'd ever said.

Passionately she pressed my face with both hands. Her violet eyes shone in the bright starlight.

"To fall in love with a Roman soldier would be impossible, wouldn't it?"

"Impossible. Absolute folly even if it happened!" I declared.

"Then we must forget this hour or two, Julius."

"I'll make the pretense."

"Pretense?"

"It can be no more than that now."

Thunderstruck, I heard her reply, "Nor for me either. That's why it must end here, and quickly."

"Yes, quickly. Before I try to find and kill the gods who brought me a woman I can never have."

Her tears dampened my face as we kissed. The pain of it was too great; we soon broke apart. I accompanied her to the chariot. She mounted the car while I hitched the team tethered nearby. The last I saw, the chariot was flying down the road to the lights of Lentini, Cynthia's dark hair streaming behind it.

My bitterness was complete. For a moment—one brief, supreme moment—I had touched glory.

And had been burned for my presumption.

# CHAPTER IV

# *DECISION OF THE SENATE*

Although search parties galloped all along the road during the night and the following day, and beaters even entered the ash grove, I remained safely hidden in a cave she had pointed out before she left. At dusk I set out toward the camp, in the direction of Syracuse. After a full circle of the sun I arrived, my legs aching from the long hike over rough ground. Torches gleamed in the tent streets. A gate guard whom I knew goggled at me:

"We thought your patrol had disappeared into the hands of the Greeks!"

"So we did. I'm the only left to tell about it. What's the meaning of all the hullabaloo?—wagons everywhere—there hasn't been so much clatter in months."

"The consul's army is landing on the beaches tonight. The commander's here already. Yonder, where the standards shine—that's his pavilion. Marcus Claudius Marcellus himself."

"What about Varro?"

"Packing to sail home on the next tide. He's been dismissed, and I say good riddance."

Hope beat high in my heart: "Then perhaps we're to be allowed to serve again?"

"Oh, I doubt that. The officers with Marcellus have stated he's using our encampment just because it's already built." His look changed to puzzlement. "Come to think of it, the officer I spoke with asked after you. He seemed to know you."

The wind had suddenly become chill. "Did he give his name?"

"No, but he was a tall, haughty sort. Obviously a noble. He had a stiff left leg."

Turning, I walked on with a mingling of fear and hatred in my heart. Sardus Pulvius had carried out his avowed plan. He had returned to the army with no loss of face. And the dark gods who raised impossible walls between me and the Lady Cynthia had cast his lot with mine again. There could be no good end to it—

Well, there was no escaping what must be done, either. I went straightaway to the pavilion of the new commander. There I spoke with the centurion, who said to me:

"He's with a delegation of your local legionnaires already. But, I suppose your news of what happened in Lentini is more pressing. Enter." He drew the hanging to one side.

Heads turned and armor flashed. Several officers gaped, Terence among them. A man seated in the commander's chair rose suddenly, glaring from beneath grizzled brows.

He had a broad, craggy face, forthright eyes and a confident manner. His thick arms bore faint scars, as well they might. Marcus Claudius Marcellus had distinguished himself in Cisalpine Gaul long ago. Single-handed, he'd slain the rebel chief of the Insubres, Britomartus, himself, and brought the warrior's ceremonial armor back to Rome nailed to an old tree trunk—exactly as he had sworn to do.

"May I ask the meaning of this intrusion, soldier?" he demanded in a harsh voice.

"I am the sub-centurion Linus Julius, General. Returned on foot from Lentini."

Apparently he knew the situation; his anger moderated:

"Ah. The vanished patrol. Where are the rest?"

"Dead." I said.

Marcellus gnawed at his underlip, then turned to the gathered officers. All of them belonged to our two exiled legions. Addressing both them and me, the commander rumbled:

"At the moment of your arrival, Linus Julius, I was being petitioned by these men who were formerly commanded by Varro. They wish to serve in the line when we attack Syracuse, rather than as garrison soldiers— the duty specified by the terms of their exile."

"To their request I'll add my own," I declared. "I also want the chance to fight."

"Exactly what happened in Lentini to generate such wrath?"

Rapidly I told him.

His eyes grew all the more dark. "Now I understand your reasons. Well, I promise you this much. The Greeks shall be repaid."

Then Marcellus proceeded to address the officers:

"And since my orders are explicit, I am not only willing but anxious to use every possible fighting man. The Republic is struggling for her life. We have the Carthaginian hosts on the run in Latium, but Hannibal's wily. Just when we think we've boxed him in, he eludes us. Without provisions from overseas, he'll be less powerful. Therefore Syracuse must be captured, and promptly. So I will not merely overlook the past—Cannae is two years dead and better forgotten anyway. I'll dispatch tablets to the Senate requesting that the exiled legions be reinducted to fight beside the men I brought on my galleys. With luck, you'll all serve the standard of Rome again. And soon."

With a lusty cheer the officers hailed the general's decision. Moments later I was swept out of the pavilion with Terence pounding my back joyously. The only cloud on the immediate horizon was Pulvius. I was sure he was already busy spreading false tales about me.

Yet the effort must have proved fruitless. In the intervening weeks, as the wagonloads of siege equipment toiled up the steep road from the lonely shingles of the Sicilian coast, no threat from him presented itself. Nor did I see him except once, at a distance, riding haughtily beside the commander on an inspection tour.

We sent lookouts to the beach to keep watch for a message galley from Rome. When the ship finally arrived, we knew it long before Marcellus rode into our camp at nightfall and sounded the ceremonial trumpets to assemble us.

Beside me, Terence's face was strained with anxiety. The next few moments would reveal whether we were again honorable men, or still disgraced. The drummer beat a tattoo for silence—

Marcellus, astride his great armored bay horse, said in a loud voice, "I have the answer you've been awaiting." Without ceremony he unlatched the tablets and began to read, his eyes expressionless:

" 'It is the opinion of the Conscript Fathers that for purposes of the Sicilian campaign, the services of publicly condemned cowards now serving in the army of the Republic are not required.' "

An audible gasp raced around the assembled ranks. Next to me, Terence let out a gasp. His face settled into bitter regret, just as mine must have done.

# CHAPTER V

# CHALLENGE

In the front ranks, a whisper and a mutter began; an ugly undercurrent in which embittered cursing soon became audible. The reaction brought Marcellus's grizzled eyebrows together in a scowl.

"May I have your attention?" he asked in a peremptory way. "At least do me the courtesy of allowing me to read the entire tablet!"

"What for?" someone cried. "Just to hear ourselves condemned?"

A peculiar, amused light shone in the general's gray eyes. I exchanged puzzled looks with Terence. In the circumstances, the commander's smile seemed more like the nasty sort of amusement a Pulvius would feel over someone's downfall.

Marcellus cleared his throat, then resumed reading:

" 'However, since the Conscript Fathers have

granted you complete authority in the conduct of the Sicilian campaign, such a decision may be left to your discretion. We will rely on your prudence and judgment.' "

He closed the tablets and handed them down to an aide. In the stunned silence, with the torches streaming out in the night wind, we understood the unconcealed amusement of a moment ago. Nevertheless, he spoke again:

"In other words, legionnaires, the Conscript Fathers have not changed their opinion of you—although I'm sure the faction of Torquatus had something to do with the wording of those tablets. The Senate, however, is not fighting this war. I am. Therefore I give you back your swords. Not as dress ornaments or play-toys, but to be used against a Greek enemy."

The cheering was well-nigh thunderous.

I was reassigned to my former position as *praefectus equitum*. In consequence, instead of drilling on foot as I'd done for two years, I had a saddle under me again. I had some authority as well. Once more the drill ground echoed to the rattle of hoofs, and the sun flashed on bright armor when I took my men out every morning to practice away their rustiness at wheeling in rank, charging and forming a mounted wedge.

Quite frequently, officers from Marcellus's staff cantered past to inspect our drill. Several days after the return to full service, I again had my men out working when I spied a familiar figure jogging toward me on a massive chestnut. The riding gear included special long stirrups. The one on the right was tucked up, empty, for he fancied himself a good enough rider not to need it. But straight as a log, his left leg hung far down below his horse's barrel.

He pulled up a short distance from where I sat my mount. I was issuing orders: *"Wheel—about! Wheel—about!* Close in between first and second, you're sloppier than hogs on horseback!"

Carefully I watched the seated figure from the corner of my eye. In no circumstances must I allow my temper to be rubbed the wrong way, else I might draw punishment that would again snatch me from active duty. Yet when I heard the jingling of Pulvius's trappings as he rode forward, I knew it would be no easy thing to converse with him.

The black spark in those bitter eyes certified my judgment. He gazed at me a moment, then said:

"Does it feel pleasant to sit on a horse after so long a time, Master Julius?"

"Yes, sir, it does," I said, eyes front so I could observe the troops wheeling again.

He affected a wounded tone: "Come now! Why the honorifics? Why call me sir? We're better friends than that."

"The past is done. Even if it were not, this isn't the time or place to recall it—"

"The past done?" He gave a hitch to his cripped left leg. His stirrup metal clinked. "Why, the past is never done, my friend—only put back on the shelf awhile, to be taken down again at the proper moment. What is really making you so timid, Master Julius? Is it truly the general order forbidding personal feuds—or your astonishment at seeing me ride again?"

Angrily I kicked my horse around so I faced him. "Put up your knives, I won't be provoked."

"Why not?" he asked in a sly way. "Are you afraid you've lost your talent for racing? I thought I'd lost mine until I got up in the saddle again. With this

137

gear—" He patted the long stirrup, "—I find that I do well enough. Quite well enough to try you again."

Unbelieving, I stared at him. The scarlet plume of his helmet danced in the morning breeze.

"Is there no end to the hate, Pulvius? Does it go on forever, like time itself?"

"Naturally not." His lips smiled but his voice was low and deadly. "It ends when I expose you for the common dung you are."

My temper grew uncontrollable:

*"Wasn't Nara enough? Didn't that satisfy you?"*

His reply sounded almost bemused: "Ah—Nara." A cloaked shoulder lifted, as if he were flicking off an insect. "Poor girl. She killed herself before she half began to enjoy the treats I'd planned for her amusement and gratification—in many ways she was a delicious little slut, wasn't she?"

The expected emotions rushed through me:

Stunning sorrow at hearing the news.

Then piercing relief that she hadn't endured too much refined torture at the hands of this monster.

Next I grieved because she had misguidedly taken the wrong path to what she presumed was security—

And of course I experienced the memory of her wonderful sweetness in my arms when she'd harbored me near the highroad, after Cannae. I bitterly regretted that our last hour of lovemaking in Rome had been so tense and angry—

But the emotion I felt sharpest of all was the hatred I bore Sardus Pulvius.

I controlled it with great effort, pointing to the mounted men on the field. They were resting their horses, awaiting further orders.

"I have work to do with those men," I said. "I beg to be excused—"

Pulvius reached across and snared my bridle. My horse pawed and stamped but the knight held fast:

"Then we don't race again a last time, Master Julius?"

"No, we do not. I know how to win your game, Pulvius. By not swallowing your bait."

"I admit nothing would displease me more than to see you, among all the cowards of Cannae, win back a respected place in the army. On the other hand, I think that will matter little, once word passes that you refuse to run against me. You see, I've already taken the liberty of telling a group of high-ranking officers—in private, of course—that you expressed a wish to try again. Your name will be on every tongue when I announce that you drew back. In fear—?"

Looking hard into his black eyes, I felt the dam of my temper burst:

"That is one thing no man says about me! When will it be—and where?"

"The drill ground here," he replied in a surprisingly cheery tone. "Shall we say an hour after nightfall? The sky promises a full moon. There should be light enough for me to see you fail."

And with that, he galloped away.

As such things do, news of the impending race spread through the camp by word of mouth. Of course the whole affair was entirely illegal, and participants as well as spectators would be punished if discovered.

Yet at least a hundred enlisted men and officers gathered like phantoms on the far side of the drill ground an hour after dark. As Pulvius had promised, the moon was full and bright. An eerie wind rippled the grass. Pulvius was already waiting with a small party of sycophants—smirking young noblemen who passed jokes behind their hands at my expense. I arrived riding the horse I had picked with care—a fleet little mare with no stamina for great distances, but a good heart and a taste for short sprints.

Pulvius greeted me with polite formality: *"Ave,* Julius! I believe we are ready."

"Let there be no dangers of interruption," I told him, my heart knocking hard in my chest. "Post some men in yonder screen of beeches, in case anyone comes from camp." Although we were partially hidden from the sprawling tent city, noise would carry.

"Already done," was his answer. "What do you say to a course down to that monument boulder in the distance? Then we'll circle it and come back here to finish."

"Agreeable."

I noticed that my mare was nervous. Then I realized he'd been unusually glib about the proposed course. Had he scouted it, hoping to gain some advantage?

To raise that question would be to cast doubts on my own courage. I was fearful of the coming encounter, but I would not let the cloaked and silent watchers know. Among them, to my dismay, I saw the churlish face of Rufio. He seemed to be paying particular attention to the obvious bad feeling between Pulvius and myself. And he was smiling.

Purses jingled. Men whispered odds and placed wagers. "Yes, there's money changing hands," Pulvius said, as if reading my thoughts. "Have you any further questions?"

"No. We're both familiar with the true stakes in this race."

Lightly he slapped his crippled leg. "So we are, dung-soldier. So we are."

And with a flamboyant gesture, he turned his mount's head toward a centurion busy marking a starting stripe with the point of his sword.

Pulvius cantered over to the stripe, unfastened the clasp of his cloak, and called:

"Ready here. The course is to that monument boulder and back to this line."

I threw my helmet on the ground and rode up beside him. The centurion raised his sword:

"When the blade falls, that is the signal."

"Agreed," I said.

"Agreed," Pulvius repeated. His confident smile unnerved me all the more. I had been out of a saddle for more than two years—and he, I was certain, had been preparing for almost as long.

# CHAPTER VI

# CONTEST

The tall nobleman rode the same chestnut he'd been mounted on earlier in the day. A white-eyed, angry-looking gelding, it was. Beside it, my own mare seemed far too light and fragile.

Moonlight glittered on the centurion's upraised blade. The sword made a white streak as he directed it down:

*"Go!"*

My mare broke forward the moment I gave her the signal. The chestnut, on the other hand, balked and reared because Pulvius kicked him too viciously.

The mare stretched her legs and galloped down the moonlit grass. Behind, I could hear cries of dismay from my rival's toadies. Pulvius cursed ferociously, finally forcing his mount into the race. A steady drumming rose over the thud of my own mare's hoofs.

The mare gave all her splendid heart to the dash down the ghostly silver plain toward the tall monument boulder looming larger and larger. By the time I had covered two-thirds of the distance to the stone marking the halfway point, the mare and I seemed to have joined together into one perfectly functioning unit.

Then from my right eye I caught a hellish glimpse of a great head thrusting forward, and a wild mane streaming out. Pulvius began to pull up alongside.

He was riding closer beside me than I liked. Bent into the wind, his face had the starkness of a silver death mask.

The monument towered against the sky now. My mare was on the inside, closest to it. Pulvius was keeping up, having brought out a little quirt with which he lashed the chestnut cruelly.

I tightened the rein to prepare for the lightning turn around the rock. Both horses answered command, slowing and wheeling at the same time. I had become conscious of man and beast on my right suddenly growing huge and black. Pulvius was crowding me, hoping to force my mare to stumble as we rounded the rock.

Halfway through the turn now. I could smell the hot reek of lathered hides. Dimly above the shriek of the wind, I heard a yelp of hurt from the chestnut; Pulvius was driving him where he did not want to go. I smashed my boot heels into the mare's barrel.

She must have sensed the peril. She seemed to leap from under me. Suddenly we were through the dangerous place, with no rocks to the left, just open plain.

The black clump of watching men began to grow in size. Pulvius had tried to unseat me. My knotted belly warned that he might do so again. The plain seemed to

144

flow by as in a silvered dream. The mare was straining to her limit. She pulled a length in front of Pulvius' horse.

But the chestnut's hoofs still beat like merciless drums. Once more he made a bid to overtake me. It was difficult to watch the terrain and my enemy at the same time. That was the reason I nearly missed what he wanted me to miss—the black crookedness that meant a little gully winding in the silver grass directly ahead.

We were still far enough from the finish line for the legionnaires to miss what happened next. Failing at the monument rock, Pulvius must have known that he might win here; the gully wound off to our left; I could not gallop wide of it unless I wanted to give him an edge I could never regain.

The chestnut's head appeared close to my shoulder, bobbing frantically. Pulvius jerked the rein and plied the whip to urge greater effort from the poor beast. The dried creek neared with every second, every heartbeat—

Suddenly the chestnut jarred my mare's flank. Pulvius's stiff left leg, a powerful weapon in such a circumstance, smashed into the mare's barrel. I felt her tremble and miss stride.

Again Pulvius crashed against us. By masterful horsemanship he pulled away instantly to avoid entanglement. The mare was now definitely off stride, heading for the gully at an oblique angle. She was off her balance and fighting to keep from falling. One more of those jolts from Pulvius and we would be in the gully with both of our necks broken—

Yet he would not stop. There was madness on his

145

face as he leaned forward in his special saddle and prepared to hit again. The second his chestnut lunged at us, I signalled the mare with a rein and heel. She jerked her head back. I thanked the gods that animals sometimes understand danger better than men—

She jumped; high and wide.

She struck the earth across the gully, running in stride and at the same time nearly snapping my neck. I heard a wild animal scream; a high-pitched curse. Savagely, I reined up—

Pulvius' charge had carried him a hair's breadth too far. The chestnut pawed the open air above the gully.

For one awful second I saw horse and rider tangled in a writhing mass against the moon. Then, with another ghastly scream from a foaming muzzle, the chestnut tumbled.

Pulvius was hurled from the saddle as the horse fell. He hung head down, his leg still caught in the special stirrup. His race was done, but not the consequences. The watchers had finally seen; they came running.

In the ditch, the chestnut was trying to free himself. I heard Pulvius shriek with pain. The chestnut's frantic hoofs struck sparks from rocks. In their madness those hoofs struck flesh as well.

I was the first to reach the gully. The gear had come untangled. The chestnut, unhurt except for its fright, was up and fleeing from the disaster. Pulvius, as hurt men often do, had strange strength; he used it to haul himself upward—

Only then did I see that he no longer had a face.

From ear to ear what had been a face was a blood-streaming mask with eyes. The thrashing hoofs had torn his flesh to pieces. If he ever lived, he would be a ghoul.

"His mount stumbled," I panted to the man who ran up.

Bile rose in my throat. Pulvius had been punished by his own doing, so I had no reason to tell of his treachery.

The centurion stared, then mumbled, "A black business." He tried to support Pulvius by the shoulder. "Sir? Sir, can you hear me? Take my arm. We'll find a surgeon."

"Find me the soldier!" he screamed. *"Find me the soldier!"*

I will never forget the sight of him that way, blinded by his own blood and baying his hatred into the night. Abruptly big Rufio was among those jostling at my elbow. He smiled and whispered:

"Now there will be two of us thinking of you. Two, that is, if Pulvius lives and you aren't charged with his murder."

Before I could answer, he shoved by and joined the party making a litter of cloaks to carry the nobleman back to camp. Pulvius had fainted at last, bloody face turned up to the moon.

By ones and twos, the watchers drifted away, not speaking. I did not sleep all that night.

At daylight I sent a lesser officer to inquire at the surgeon's tent. He came back to report that Pulvius was alive, though his head was wrapped in linen and the doctors despaired of what he would look like in the future. Indeed, the doctors did not know whether he *had* a future.

From camp gossips I soon picked up the explanation for the tragedy: Pulvius maintained he had been riding alone when the accident took place. In a way I had expected some such fabrication. To have brought the race into the open would have imperilled him, for if I were accused of attempted murder, I could not have kept silent about his tricks. As it was, I almost wished him dead. Once he recovered—if he did—his hate would be stronger than ever.

Fortunately for my sanity, Marcellus chose those days to begin his campaign against Sicily. Another great fleet of ninety galleys was due soon from the Roman shipyards, to begin the attack on Syracuse by sea as well as land. How it would fare, no one could say. For months, rumors had circulated that the port had always been impregnable because of certain gigantic war engines invented by an ancient Greek mathematician, one Archimedes. He was a kinsman of the dead tyrant Hiero, and still lived in the city, so the story ran. The tale-tellers maintained the machines were ten times larger and more powerful than anything we had, and were even now stored somewhere in the catacombs under the port's imposing buildings.

I soon learned Marcellus considered the machines fictions, however; bogeys to frighten the credulous, and therefore not worthy of his worry. So until the flotilla arrived to begin the final siege of Syracuse, the general intended to repay the Greeks at Lentini for the murder of three Romans. At the same time, he would be reducing a strategic garrison.

My *ala* was chosen to ride with the cohorts given that assignment. As we moved out on a chill gray day, I was grateful to leave the camp behind. Pulvius was

148

up and about again, a far greater threat to me than the Greeks toward whom we rode.

But there was danger enough remaining at Lentini, as I discovered when we went against its walls.

# CHAPTER VII

# WARNING FOR MARCELLUS

Four days and four nights, the walls of Lentini withstood the stones and scrap metal and firepots hurled against them by the *ballistae* and the catapults operated by Marcellus's engineers. The role of the cavalry would be crucial only when the walls crumbled; then, mounted men would sweep in ahead of the cohorts on foot. So for me those first four days were relatively idle.

We camped in the hills above the town, watching pillars of sooty smoke rise from the burning buildings and making poor jokes about the frantic Greeks scurrying to shore up breaks in the walls. My mind was not really focused on the attack; instead, it wandered in some limbo where I saw a Greek widow's lovely violet eyes, felt her tears on my cheeks, and her lips on my own.

On the second day, bands of peasants began to drift down out of the higher hills. They were coarsely dressed, black-haired men led by a chief named Malthuso. These Sicilians had long been required to pay exorbitant tribute to their Greek overlords. Now they offered their services to Marcellus. He accepted, especially since they'd brought their own weapons—scythes; hunting spears; wicked sheep-skinning knives.

The battering of the walls finally wrought irreperable damage. On the fourth night Marcellus called a conference of his officers. He unrolled maps of the town, indicating three points at the outer wall:

"At each of these locations, we will make a concerted attack at first light. The walls have been shored up at least twice in all three places, but my reports indicate the work's been hastily done. Senior commanders are to move mantlets and scaling ladders forward during the night—" His hand moved on. "Cavalry units will be stationed at these two main gates, ready to ride in when the first legionnaries go over the top and reach the gates from within. The foot will seize the gates and hold them open."

"And then," said Malthuso, the peasant leader, "we'll take back some of what's been stolen from us. I saw my cousin butchered by those damned Greek soldiers. I've waited a long time for this moment—"

At dawn, which was chill and misting, I found myself at the front of my troop, waiting in a grove just a short gallop from the western gates. Already the Greeks were on the walls. They fired crossbows and cast down javelins. Somewhere the siege engines rumbled, and occasionally I caught a crash of falling masonry. Since the main points of the engineering attack were hidden from us by the terrain, we would have to rely on bugle signals.

At last I heard three clear piping notes. The gates had been seized and opened. I raised my sword!

"Forward—*full gallop!*"

We rode into the town, many of the men shouting joyously at the prospect of death for our enemies. Many of those same men fell, for the garrison had by no means given up. I saw one of my best riders take an arrow in the guts. I saw another's head severed cleanly from his body, and the head strike the earth and settle near his open right palm so that in death he looked as if he were offering part of himself to the enemy.

But the Greeks died too; limbs were chopped off, eyes gouged out before death or afterwards. Men lay in ditches, pleading for a merciful release which I myself granted in three instances. Soon my sword dripped red.

Despite the stiff resistance of the Greeks, it seemed to me the outcome was inevitable. As it turned out, I was correct. Within another hour, Lentini fell.

Marcellus rode in triumphantly, preceded by six military tribunes. They sought out the commanders of each unit:

"By order of the commanding general, there shall be no looting of private homes."

"That's a fine order!" I growled. "How does Marcellus expect us to keep the men happy?"

"That's your affair, Prefect. We'll have trouble enough without our troops adding to it."

"I don't follow. Who besides the soldiers will complain?"

"Those dog-leg peasants who came under the standards. It appears their chief, Malthuso, is half a patriot and half a bandit. He and his followers are already riot-

153

ing at the eastern gate. They're furious over the looting edict. At dawn they were our allies but they aren't now. One whole cohort is engaged in driving them back into the hills—so keep your men under control and don't add to the confusion." So saying, he spurred away.

Strangely, by nightfall, when a pall of smoke hung over Lentini, it was I, not any of my men, who was ready to disobey. It happened thus:

A huge legionary mess was hastily organized on the drill ground. Out of kettles came a stew of young pig and vegetables. Discipline relaxed. The soldiers sat in small groups, laughing and boasting of the day's success. I joined one of my junior officers, thankful to be out of the saddle.

"We'd have better fare," the man with me complained, "but half the cooks are at work in yonder building." He indicated the headquarters, glowing with lamps and torches.

"Well, the commander deserves to eat in private."

"Eat, yes. But entertain the enemy like a brother? No."

I asked the junior officer what he meant.

"Simple enough. Yesterday—last night, actually—the Greek general Hippocrates slipped into Lentini to survey the defenses. He was caught before he could slip out again. Hadn't you heard that?"

"No, but come to think of it, one bragging Greek did shout at me that his commander was on the walls. Personally in charge. I never dreamed it was anyone as important as Hippocrates."

"Well, it was. They say Marcellus is treating him very cordially, too. Even plans to let him go—in my opinion that's carrying fairness a bit far. Far be it from me to try to understand the behavior of generals."

"Nor do I understand it," I said, rising quickly and putting aside my mess kit. I hesitated only a moment before heading for the headquarters building, not a little disturbed. I had remembered certain of Lady Cynthia's warnings.

After some wrangling, a senior officer agreed to fetch the general from the mess hall. I waited in the great echoing rotunda until Marcellus appeared at the head of the stairs. He recognized me and came down quickly. Through the mess hall doors I heard laughter and loud talk suitable to the aftermath of a bloody battle.

"I was told this was a most urgent matter, Prefect," the commander said. "Kindly be brief."

"Sir—" Again I hesitated. Then I counted the stakes and spoke up. "Sir, it's being said you're entertaining the commander of the Greek forces who was captured today—"

He bristled, justifiably arrogant:

"And you fancy that's your affair?"

"Sir, I—I think it may be." He colored. "Please hear me out! I have some knowledge of this Hippocrates which perhaps you do not. He is more than what he pretends to be—"

"More than the military commander of Sicily?"

"So I have reason to believe. He's the coming power in Syracuse, if in fact he doesn't rule already."

Marcellus's anger changed to amusement. "Nonsense. Young Hieronymus is king."

"In name only." But my hope was dimming; I was making a botch of it. "You may discipline me for presuming, sir, but I beg you to be wary of the enemy commander. If you can't bring yourself to kill him, then at least keep him prisoner."

Marcellus remained silent a long moment, clearly seething. At last he managed to say:

"Prefect, I find your remarks not only presumptuous and insulting, but downright incredible too. In my opinion Hippocrates is a wholly honorable man. I demand to know why you differ with that opinion."

"Because there are those in Syracuse who know your guest for what he is—an opportunist. I'm speaking of people not firmly aligned with Carthage. They can do nothing to help us because this Greek general finds it to his advantage to resist us. He has no real quarrel with us, but opposing us will help elevate him to power and—"

I stopped, dismally aware of my failure to convince him. His next retort confirmed the failure:

"I have a good mind to order you whipped for babbling nonsense. Not to mention insubordination and insolence! Unless you can prove what you're saying, I will do just that."

"Prove it, sir? Prove that in a week or a month, Hieronymus may be dead? Prove that your guest is scheming to take the place of Hieronymus? No, sir, I can't prove any of it. But I believe it's true. And if you'll just keep him prisoner, there may be no need to shed Roman blood in order to capture the port—"

In the shadowed rotunda, counterpointing laughter and the clank of cups from the hall, Marcellus' voice became a growl:

"Once more, Prefect—on what grounds do you make such statements?"

Scant though it was, I was forced to offer the only proof in my possession:

"I was told about Hippocrates by a person in a position to know."

*"What* person?"

"The Greek's own half-sister. The woman whose chariot I discovered on the road."

He had heard part of that tale already. But I repeated it, omitting only Lady Cynthia's role in freeing me, for after my escape, I had tried to protect her by stating that certain Greek-hating citizens of Lentini were responsible for my release. Lady Cynthia's appraisal of her half-brother I gave Marcellus whole, however. I only made it sound as if she had told me about him when I came to her assistance in the rain.

For a moment an odd light appeared in his eyes. "Interesting," he murmured, a shade less testy than before. But his curiosity submerged beneath renewed anger and scorn; he shook his head sharply and snapped, "But how is it she unburdened herself to you? A Roman?"

"No doubt—" I found myself stammering. "—no doubt she was grateful to me, and—and she is one of those who would not oppose our capture of the port—"

He snorted; a sound curiously like a trap snapping shut:

"But it comes down to *gratitude?* Prefect, you're naive. Did it never occur to you that perhaps this woman bears some secret grudge against her half-brother? Did it never occur to you that her story might be deliberately colored?"

"General, I know the woman! I know she told the truth, I—"

"You can claim that on the strength of one encounter?" he exclaimed. "Then you're a fool. And for bothering me with your fancies, I think you deserve something more appropriate than whipping. You should be required to confront this alleged schemer in person."

With a flick of the napkin he indicated the staircase.

"Kindly precede me back into the banquet hall. *At once!*"

# CHAPTER VIII

# *ACCUSED*

No walk in my life was as long and agonizing as that one into the lamplit hall. Staff officers put down their wine and turned to stare. Worst of all, in the silence I heard Marcellus say to himself, "Oh no, most impossible!" Then he chuckled. Was I the madman?

Seated in a curved chair at the highest table was a Greek of about forty years. He had a thrusting jaw, a bold nose and a generally strong face marred only by dark eyes set too close together. He was leaning over as if sharing a jest with the armored Roman next to him. They seemed on the best of terms.

"General?" Marcellus boomed, reaching for a wine cup and sloshing down its contents. "I hope you won't consider it a slur if I report that in my camp certain very humorous tales are being circulated about you—"

Marcellus let out a soft belch. I stood hot-cheeked

and humiliated. A sudden stillness descended in the hall. Hippocrates blinked.

"Tales, my good Marcellus? What sort of tales?" His tone was casual; brotherly. Only in the quick, calculating glance that he threw me did I see his alarm.

Marcellus grinned. "Tales saying I'd do well to treat you as an enemy. Tales warning me that you're something more than a rival officer whom the fortunes of war have temporarily cast in the loser's role—"

*Damn him!* I thought. I had welcomed the general's fairness when the Senate might have swayed him against allowing the exiled legions to serve with honor. But now that same sense of fair play was blinding him to all reality.

"This prefect, right here," he continued, "is the man who aided your sister when her chariot overturned. He tells me I shouldn't treat you as a fellow officer but as a prisoner since you and not Hieronymus control Sicily. Apparently you half-sister told him so. Incredible, eh?"

Hippocrates feigned amused astonishment. "Incredible indeed, Marcellus. And this is the man who says such things about me—?"

"The man who escaped from Lentini!" I cried, having concluded I'd be totally finished if I showed weakness. "The other three were tortured to death by your men!"

Even at that he didn't anger, though for an instant I thought I detected venom in his glance. If so, it was quickly hidden. "Spare me," he said in a gentle voice, raising one hand. "I had nothing to do with that. I neither practice nor condone butchery."

He turned to our commander, continuing in an urbane yet faintly contemptuous tone: "Esteemed Marcellus! Obviously my role on this island once more requires clarification. As I have been at some pains to explain long before this, I am responsible to King Hieronymus just as you are responsible to your Senate. I am a professional soldier, not a politician. The functions of the latter, I leave where they belong. So please understand—it was Hieronymus who declared for Carthage, not I. And despite what my half-sister implied to this man, I have no control over our monarch—"

He eyed me with a cool gaze again. "I think I can guess why she might have said such things, however." He leaned forward, with a trace of a smirk showing. "It's come to my attention that my sister was smitten with some nameless fellow she met in Lentini. I questioned her about it but she would say little. Now suppose this is the man. He would surely know I'd disapprove of Cynthia consorting with him—a person of his low rank. Knowing that, perhaps he decided to spite me. Spread imbecilic stories such as the one I've just heard—"

Slowly, the smile widened. "But we are all gentlemen here. With one exception. We are sophisticated enough to understand such a foolish trick—"

The smile vanished. "Which, I must say, nevertheless annoys me."

Flushing, Marcellus said, "I offer my humblest apologies! I thought hearing it might amuse you."

"To the contrary. It makes me wonder whether your courtesy is genuine, or merely a ruse whose purpose I can't yet discern."

He was a clever one, impugning Marcellus' honor that way, and at the same time making our commander, not himself, the target of suspicion. Beet-faced, Marcellus cried:

"I assure you I've acted in good faith!"

Hippocrates' reply was a doubtful shrug.

That upset Marcellus even more. He spun on me:

*"Take yourself out of my sight, Prefect!"*

Turning a trembling back, he mounted to the high table, where he immediately began placating his guest with polite words. Sickened and ashamed, I started to leave. Before I reached the door, cursing myself for not realizing that the rules which allowed enemy generals to fraternize like brothers did not apply to common soldiers, I was struck by the sight of a face watching mine. Unnoticed before, the face seemed to leap out from among a party of new arrivals; officers who had ridden in late in the day to administer the occupation.

Once, the face had been human. Now it was a crisscross of welts and white scars, hideous to behold. One whole side was still bandaged.

Watching me, Pulvius popped an olive into his mouth. Then he turned to a companion and smiled as if I did not exist.

I awakened in my assigned place in the Greek barracks shortly before daybreak, hearing the thud of boots and seeing pale lanterns swinging. Half a dozen guards headed by a tribune went from pallet to pallet.

"Where is the prefect Linus Julius? Wake up, you!"

"No, not this one, Tribune. Down the line. There."

With a cold heart I rose and confronted the tribune. "I am Linus Julius."

"Then it is my sorrowful duty to place you under arrest."

Had the wrath of Marcellus exploded during the night? "On what charge?" I asked him.

"A most unfortunate one. Shortly after leaving Lentini at midnight, the Greek commander Hippocrates

162

and his honor guard were attacked on the highway by armed men. The general was nearly killed. He was guaranteed safe conduct. Marcellus has sent for you."

"I haven't stirred from this barracks—! Well, not since I returned, anyway—"

My voice had faltered for good reason. Last night after the shameful scene in the hall, I had talked a while with Terence. After he'd gone off to bed, I had walked an hour or more in the dark, misty streets, keeping to myself and avoiding the posted watchmen.

"Well, it's a matter for the general," the tribune replied, not wanting the burden. "You can explain to him."

And so I did. But by then, I knew the wheel of fate was turning to crush me. By no remarkable coincidence, Pulvius was with the commander when I was brought in.

"I had nothing to do with it," I told him. "Your tribune said it was a band of men, not a solitary assassin."

"True," Marcellus replied with a grave nod. "One of the guards I assigned to Hippocrate's train saw armor, however. Roman armor."

"It must have been Malthuso and the peasants you sent away. They were in a bad mood over their ill-treatment. Perhaps one of them stole the armor before he left Lentini—"

"Or perhaps," Pulvius intervened softly, "you were with them, Linus Julius. The hate you bore the Greek general because of his half-sister was painfully apparent in the disgusting scene last night. And the tribune who brought you in did some checking on your whereabouts later. You were gone from barracks a long time. For a Prefect of Horse to slip through the gates is no trick at all."

He turned to Marcellus, twisting the knife:

"I think we must be more than casually suspicious, General."

"I agree." His gloomy gaze shifted to me. "Pending an investigation, you are to be locked up. You should thank the gods the immediate punishment's no worse. Had Hippocrates been injured, I, who promised him safe conduct, would be forced to kill you on the spot."

Thus I tasted the world's justice again. A trumped-up charge—but in no time at all I was clapped in prison.

# CHAPTER IX

# FRIENDSHIP'S PRICE

I sat in the cell through the night and reflected on the ridiculous charge which had been made against me. There was no way anyone could prove I had hated Hippocrates enough to steal out and join men bent on killing him. Yet there was no way I could disprove it, either.

But what was the object of the whole business? That was the central, unfathomable riddle.

I knew that Pulvius's hand had no doubt been working behind the scenes, pointing the way to my guilt for a receptive Marcellus. Although I didn't know what twists the scheme might yet take, somehow I sensed a deeper threat than a mere desire to harass and embarass me. Pulvius's hate would not be so lightly satisfied.

Early next morning I was again summoned before

the commander. Though he was obviously in better humor, having presumably slept, he still did not look at me with any cordiality. Nor did he look at Pulvius—but that was understandable.

The crippled patrician lounged beside a narrow window embrasure, gray morning light illuminating the unbandaged half of his scarred face. A deliberate pose? I wondered. Was it meant to remind me—to remind me—?

Marcellus pushed aside several tablets into whose wax he'd been inscribing orders with his stylus. "This morning we shall inquire further into the unfortunate occurrence on the highroad. After consuming a great deal of wine at the banquet, I confess I was not thinking too clearly."

His moderate tone gave me cause for hope. I kept silent. It was Pulvius who stepped forward and spoke:

"I also admit to acting immoderately." His back was to the general, and his words were sweet as honey. But his eyes mocked me. "In truth, I was the one who suggested that you might be the guilty person, Prefect—and I did it solely because some armor was glimpsed by our men who fought off the attackers—"

Marcellus broke in: "Last evening we discussed the death penalty. Now, however, a soldier has come forward with information tending to support your innocence and overturn our rather hasty conclusions. I must add, however, that the information is rather unsavory."

Pulvius plodded toward a curtained doorway. "Shall I bring the man in, sir?"

The general nodded. He seemed embarrassed. His cheeks shone pink, and he was perspiring.

The man who walked into the chamber, feigning cow-eyed discomfort, was Rufio.

"What about the tribune Terence?" Pulvius asked. "I have him in the antechamber—"

Marcellus gnawed his lips. "You might as well fetch him in too. Nastiness or not, the prefect's life is at stake."

While I watched in stunned, confused silence, a guard accompanied gray-haired Terence through the door, gripping his arm. Terence threw off the restraint. His face was composed as he raised his hand to salute his commander. But the outstretched fingers shook a little. More than ever, I smelled some sort of a trap.

Like a magistrate, Pulvius began to limp up and down. Rufio stood at attention, eyes on the ceiling and helmet in the crook of his arm. Marcellus turned towards the window, shielding his eyes with his hand as though the whole matter was somehow too unpleasant to bear.

Pulvius spoke in a measured, emotionless way:

"In the process of searching for witnesses who might have seen Linus Julius within the walls at the approximate hour Hippocrates' honor guard was being attacked, it is our regret that we have located one." He indicated Rufio, then he peered at Terence. "Are you acquainted with the crime of which your friend is charged, Tribune?"

"I am," Terence replied, his tone polite but aloof. "It is my opinion he could not possibly have done it."

Pulvius sighed.

"Perhaps it's more than an opinion, eh? Although I ordinarily despise those who spy on others, in this case Rufio may be forgiven. His testimony will save Linus Julius. No doubt the hill people *were* resentful of not

167

being able to loot freely. No doubt they *did* set upon the first Romans who chanced along the highroad last night. Perhaps they didn't even know whom they were attacking. And finally, the armor one of the guards saw was no doubt stolen. Because—"

Here he licked his lips almost daintily.

"—because, you see, Rufio has reported that he *knows* Linus Julius could not have left Lentini to join the attackers."

He was facing Terence now, his voice soft and yet accusing:

"In a deserted part of the former Greek barracks, Rufio—unobserved—saw you and your Greek lover. What the two of you were doing was hardly masculine."

Terence turned white. Sourness boiled up in my mouth. "That is the vilest accusation—" I began. Rufio's eyes flicked toward me and I understood:

He hated me. And he knew that Pulvius hated me—hadn't he been in the crowd at the moonlight race when Pulvius ruined his face trying to kill me?

Which one had hatched this filthy plot—which one had first broached it to the other, once my blunder in the banquet hall set the stage—I did not know. Nor did I care. The surprise attack by the peasants had provided their opportunity—perhaps sooner than they'd ever anticipated.

Marcellus lifted his hand from his brow. "Now do you understand, Prefect, why this pains me, Linus Julius?"

"It pains us all," Pulvius sighed piously. "Greek love is a disgusting practice." Staring intently at Terence, he continued, "To place an officer of your spotless reputation in such a compromising position is not an easy

168

task for us, Tribune. Nevertheless, I think you see the situation. I trust that your—ah—friendship for Linus Julius will lead to the truth, however unpleasant. Otherwise—" He shrugged. "We cannot be certain the prefect was not among the attackers."

Silence. Terence's face was like marble.

"This man Rufio," he said quietly, "is telling the truth."

*"In the name of the gods, Terence!"* I cried. *"You know why they are doing this! Don't perjure yourself!"*

Terence refused to look at me. "My friend could not have possibly taken part in the attack on the Greek general's party," he continued. "We were together. All night."

"As lovers?" Pulvius persisted. "As *Greek* lovers?"

"Yes."

"I will not stand by and let him ruin himself on my account!" I shouted.

The hand of Marcellus struck his own thigh, loudly. "Silence! The facts are out and the case is closed—though I prefer not to think at what price. I'm glad treachery and hatred did not carry you out to that highroad last night, Linus Julius. Yet I can't conceal the fact that I'm disappointed and sickened to learn the truth in this way. Out of my sight, both of you!"

As he spoke, Rufio had been standing like a statue, at perfect attention. I looked from him to Pulvius to Terence. For the latter's sake I didn't let the yell of outrage tear out of my throat as I wanted to. I could see Terence was near the breaking point. His cheeks were pale as parchment.

Marcellus's glare bid us hurry. Numb, I started for the door. Pulvius couldn't resist a last word:

"Linus Julius, I too am pleased to see a Roman

legionary acquitted of a charge of treachery against his general. I congratulate you on winning such loyalty from your, ah, friend."

Marcellus surged to his feet, bellowing: "I said *get them out of here!*"

Terence turned and walked unsteadily in my direction. I stood aside to let him pass. His eyes were glazed.

Shaken, I followed him into the sunlight flooding the headquarter steps. He kept walking. Or better, stumbling. I stepped in front of him. He was forced to stop.

"Why did you let them do that to you, Terence? *Why?*"

A weary shrug. "If I hadn't, they might have killed you."

Anger unleashed unkindness: "Is friendship that valuable to you? So valuable you'd ruin your reputation for it?"

His straightforward answer shamed me:

"Yes, Julius, it is. We will live it down. They'll forget about it soon. Now please leave me alone for a while."

So saying, he wrapped his cloak around his arm and started across the parade ground. His step was still unsteady, and he blinked a good deal. Hate for Pulvius and Rufio consumed me again as I watched his shoulders slump lower than I had ever seen them. His trim posture was utterly destroyed.

For a man of his sensibilities, nothing could have been more shameful than the admission he'd chosen to make. I almost wished that he hadn't been so foolish; that he'd let me die. The price he'd paid—and the fact that he was *willing* to pay—were almost beyond my comprehension. In a world where men like Pulvius held power, such gestures seemed worthless.

My mind was so confused that I do not remember exactly how I came on the group of legionnaries loitering near the stables. But my daze left me when I heard a snicker:

"*Ave,* Greek!"

My cheeks burning, I whirled. "The first one who speaks—" I began in a ragged voice.

"Why aren't you in the arms of your lover?" one of them cooed. "It's such a pretty day!"

"He must come by it naturally," another said. "After all, he spends his time with horses."

"Whoresons!" I ran at them, striking out.

"Careful, Greek!" one of them snarled, pushing me back. "We wouldn't want to hurt anyone so delicate and tender as you. It might spoil you for your lover's blissful—"

His nose dissolved as I broke it with my fist; broke it and snarled like an animal, my hand slimed with blood and self-control gone.

I lashed out at another face. That enraged them, and they attacked. Still gripped by incoherent rage, I fought clumsily. It was no trick for them to pile on me and overwhelm me.

The sun seemed to spin and flare overhead. I struck the earth, pain bursting in my belly where they had hit me. A boot slammed the side of my head. Laughter, coarse and unruly, dinned and receded.

"Whoresons—" By now it was a mere croak. "Dirty, foul-tongued—"

One of the soldiers stamped on my gut. I cried out as darkness came.

171

I awakened a long time later, in the surgeon's quarters.

They gave me wine. Saw to my cuts and bruises. And realized after many questions that I would not say how I had come to be injured, or by whom. The chief surgeon's rigid expression told me he already knew many of the particulars anyway.

"If you intend to be stubborn and press no charges," he said, "that is none of my affair. However, I suppose I might as well be the one to tell you." He wiped his hands clean and tossed away the linen. Something fearful moved in his eyes.

"There was a tribune—Terence—whose name was linked with yours—"

Already I was off the stool, stalking toward him. "What about him? One remark and I'll wring your neck."

"*Hold!* I was only trying to break it to you gently."

"Was?" The word struck my mind like a delayed thunderclap. "You talk about the tribune who *was*—"

"They found the fellow an hour ago, in the barracks. Perhaps you had better go see for yourself, rather than vent your spleen on me."

"See what, damn you?"

I think he enjoyed telling me: "His body. He hanged himself."

# CHAPTER X

# LOVERS' MEETING

Day followed day in despairing succession. Unbearable guilt weighed upon me. Guilt and the knowledge that Terence had squandered his life. I was not worth what he had done. The only small satisfaction I gained in that harrowing time came from vindication of the tale I had told Marcellus about Hippocrates.

The Romans had a number of spies inside the walls of Syracuse. One reported that once Hippocrates regained the safety of the port, he lost no time in betraying Marcellus's trust. He spread stories to the populace that the Roman general had neither spared Lentini's citizens nor restrained looting, but rather had massacred a large portion of the able-bodied men of the garrison town. With Lentini occupied and Syracuse the only major city still in Greek hands, no one who heard the lies ventured out to verify them. The spy also reported that Hippocrates' harangues had spread panic among the Greeks, and further inflamed their hatred of the Republic.

At this time most of the Roman troops had returned to the hill camp, leaving a token force to occupy Lentini. That Hippocrates was not yet in full command at Syracuse was demonstrated when a truce delegation arrived at the camp. The delegation had been sent by Hieronymus.

Perhaps he feared the growing Roman force, and foresaw an all but certain siege. Or perhaps he wanted to assert his authority against what must have been a popular clamor for the strong, anti-Roman position represented by Hippocrates. At any rate, he requested a peace parley. Negotiations would be held inside the walls of Syracuse. Wonder of wonders, Marcellus consented.

Most of us under arms were stunned by his decision. Hadn't Hippocrates given our general a vicious insult by accepting his hospitality and a guard of honor, then blackening his name with lies? If all was fair in war, Marcellus had seemed to live by a different code for a while, foolishly believing Hippocrates did too. But there was soon no doubt that the general had agreed to the parley.

Preparations for the siege came to a standstill. Then we learned Marcellus would not go to Syracuse in person. He sent Sardus Pulvius.

So it was hardly pure chance when my name, with three dozen others from my troop, appeared on the roster of Pulvius's guard. He had asked for me, I was sure. I discovered the reason the morning our party prepared to ride from camp.

Pulvius had no difficulty in sitting a saddle. Only his

174

face had been injured in the racing contest. That face was a strange looming landscape of pits and ridges as he approached me on horseback, splendidly armored and suspiciously cordial:

"*Ave,* Prefect! I trust you plan to enjoy our sojourn in the Greek port—" Then came the poison behind the smile. "You seem to have an affinity for persons of Greek persuasion."

Hatred choked me again. I held it back; forced my voice to remain level:

"I will carry out my assignment, sir."

"Yes, I'm sure you will. You always were a sweet, faithful sort." Laughing, he cantered off.

As we started for the enemy city, I realized he would probably continue to bait me. I vowed not to break down under his insults. In fact, my only means of taking revenge was a certain passivity which would spoil his sport, and this I endeavored to maintain.

On the road he overlooked no opportunity to jog by and deliver himself of stinging remarks, all relating to Terence. But I gave him no satisfaction. As we dropped down through the hills toward the seacoast, a new thought began to sustain me and make his jibes a bit easier to bear:

With a little good fortune, which was surely due me at long last, I might see Cynthia again.

The opening negotiations seemed endless as well as pointless. They consisted of hours of oratory about how foolish it was to shed human blood in vain. Listening to such sentiments, I laughed silently. I was thankful to return to my assigned room when the talks broke off in late afternoon.

We were given a fine banquet in our quarters that

night. As I finished and turning my thoughts to the problem of locating Cynthia, a slave sought me out:

"Sir, you have been identified to me as Linus Julius—"

"What of it?"

"A resident of this household wishes to speak with you in his apartment." The slave showed me a small wax disc inscribed with Greek characters. "Here is your safe conduct. Follow me, please."

I did so, but I kept my hand on the hilt of my sword. I fully expected Kyron or Hippocrates to be waiting.

Instead, I was surprised when I was ushered into a dim chamber up near the roof of the labyrinthine building. The apartment was splendidly furnished, though the divans seemed dusty and disused. A large oval bench was littered with curious paraphernalia— queer globes of golden wire, fragments of parchments, maps, innumerable styli and many, many rolled-up books.

An old man came in from the balcony. He was spider-frail, and looked as though a breeze would float him away. His hair and beard were thin and white, contrasting with his dark, leather-like skin. He wore a tunic of some poor stuff, gray and woolly and utterly without character. But his small eyes, the color of walnuts, were alert and ageless.

"This is the one, hey?" he murmured, dismissing the slave with a gesture. "Well, walk in, walk in, young Roman. Contrary to popular belief, there are no evil spirits to possess you here." He chuckled. "I do confess that sometimes I am discouraged by the ignorance of some in this city. The ones who feel magic, and not natural principles, are my sole interest—" With a resigned sigh, he began to pick through the litter of apparatus, almost as if he'd already forgotten me.

"They didn't tell me whom I was summoned to see—" I began.

He turned, pleased. "Oh, you speak Greek, do you? Yes, now I recall—she told me you did. Give me a moment or two, if you please. I'm not accustomed to the role of Cupid. Playing it has disturbed my train of thought—"

He started back to his collection of curiosities. "See here," I said. "Who are you and what do you want of me?"

Instead of answering immediately, he picked up a long wooden rod and peered at it. Presently he said, "Archimedes, that's who I am. Archimedes." Lost in private musings over the rod, he did not sound at all certain. "Now just hold your peace one moment more—"

Irritated, I did so. He began to mutter softly to himself, picking up a small block of wood and laying it down again on the table. Crosswise over the block, he rested the wand. On one end of the wand he set the base of one of the wire globes.

He pressed down on the wand's free end. The wand bent on the block, but the globe tipped with a crash.

Lamplight reflected on the filaments of the globe as he picked it up and smiled vaguely. "Just imagine this globe was a world, soldier. And imagine this—" He touched the wand with his other hand. "A lever hanging in space."

"I beg your pardon, sir. The only world I know is flat."

"Nonsense. That's popular superstition, nothing more. Now pay attention! Imagine this lever hung in

177

space. I might then move the world—even though it be ten hundred times heavier than my lever!" His delighted expression faded. "But how to suspend both lever and fulcrum in heaven—that's a problem I have not solved as yet."

Such matters were beyond the scope of my limited education. Still, it *was* oddly interesting to see him tip over the golden globe with just the aid of a block and thin stick. He tried it twice more.

At one point I ventured a question: "Why should you want to do something like that at all?"

"Why, because no one has ever done it before!" The old man smiled wryly. "I suppose you'll tell me that my interest will roil the universe, and bring down wrath on my head. Perhaps it will. After all, who can be sure there isn't a convocation of gods seated in the heavens this very moment? Watching my every move with disapproval?"

"No one can be sure," I agreed.

"Nevertheless, a man must go where his mind takes him—and be prepared to accept the consequences. I give you as an example the allegorical gift of Prometheus—do you know of the legend? Yes, well, he brought fire to man and was therefore punished. But he had done what he felt was necessary. And despite his punishment, he enabled man to make progress."

"But can these inquiries of your be called progress?"

"Certainly! Knowledge *is* progress."

He spoke with profound conviction just then. Yet he still seemed to be a frail and bemused eccentric. Could he truly be the sharp-witted engineer who had invented the monster war-machines supposedly hidden somewhere in Syracuse? I recalled they said he'd designed them primarily for his kinsman's amusement, and was

178

not overly interested in their practical application—he sensed my growing impatience; cast the rod aside:

"Oh, very well. I see I'm becoming tedious with these philosophical matters. To speak plainly for a change, you are here because I am acting as intermediary for a certain lady—"

The old eyes sharpened, amused. "The lady sometimes employs my villa as a place of refuge. It's located on the sea wall in the outer quarter. Going there, she can escape from fortune-hunting swains who refuse to let her alone—"

Now I had no doubt he meant Cynthia. The old man continued:

"The lady wishes to see you. She's waiting at the villa. The slave outside—the dolt with the disc—he will escort you."

I thanked him and turned to go, only wishing with a certain bitterness that I could be so far removed from concern with wordly affairs. My regret was forgotten as the slave handed me a hooded cloak and we went stealing down the dark lanes and thoroughfares of Syracuse, proceeding through the central quarter past the inner wall to the outer section, arriving finally in a fine, prosperous street.

There, the sea wind blew briskly and I heard the distant beating of waves. The slave held up a lantern, saying he would wait to accompany me on the return journey. Then he bade me knock.

When the door opened, red hair glinted in the antechamber. "Come in, master!" the slave girl said. "It brings me joy to welcome you to this house."

She shut the outer door and held up a bronze lamp. I recognized the red-haired Daphne whom I had encountered on the high road with Cynthia. There was a

179

certain coarse prettiness to her features, but sheer animal lust shone in her eyes. Her gown was of thin, lemon-colored stuff, hardly concealing her huge breasts.

Daphne smiled a slow, lascivious smile. "Before I take you to her, I want you to know one thing, sir. Should you find her unresponsive, please be aware that I have free run of the villa. Since that day on the road I have thought of you constantly. I could bring you delights which I expect you've never experienced before—"

"Enough chatter!" I said impatiently. "Conduct me to your mistress."

She flushed. "High and mighty Roman, aren't you? I may be a slave, but there aren't many who would refuse when I—"

"I am one who will refuse," I broke in. *"Where is the lady?"*

She scowled, turned and led the way. We passed richly appointed rooms smelling of dust and full of shadow. She pulled aside a final hanging, her whisper sweetly vicious:

"Thank you for being so gracious with me, master. I shan't forget." Then she hurried away.

Cynthia was waiting on the terrace. Her arms smelled of sweet balm. Her eyes shone deep violet in the starlight. Far below the balustrade, the blue bay rippled. I found myself being unexpectedly gruff:

"Why did you send for me? Why did you bother?"

"Because I wanted to see you again!" Her body pressed tightly against mine. "Do you need more reason than that?"

"Yes. Every time I think of you, there is no joy in it.

Don't misunderstand—I—I do think highly of you. But doing so is futile, it's—"

I found I couldn't continue.

"Finish," she whispered. "Say the rest."

I leaned down, gazing into those fair, lovely eyes. "We are at war, Cynthia! Not on the same side. But much more than that separates us. Once you had a husband who had wealth and a high position. Even if we were both Greeks or both Romans, I will never have either. So how can this mean anything to you—?"

"But it does, Julius! Strangely and quickly, that night in the grove, it came to mean more than I can begin to say. How it happened, I can't explain. Who is ever able to explain love? Not even the poets, though they try and try. But you're probably right—we will never be able to share what a man and woman should. Somehow that only makes me want you all the more. When I sat on the gallery last evening—"

Astonished, I broke in, "The state banquet?"

"Yes." A trace of a mischievous smile. "You never suspected. But I was watching you—" The smile disappeared. "And your face—your face hurt me with a strange, sweet kind of hurt. That was the moment I truly knew how much I cared for you. That's why I begged Archimedes to help me arrange for the slave to guide you here. So there would at least be one more night beyond that first one—"

Eagerly and yet with a certain sorrow, she stood on tiptoe. Her lips parted, and her passion ran free and wild as her tongue when we kissed.

My arms circled her waist. I held the gentle naked warmth of her, hidden from me by only the thinnest of materials. Soon she pulled away, hurried across the ter-

181

race, and closed the hangings separating us from the main house.

Then, as if making an offering, she unfastened the onyx clip at her left shoulder.

The gown fell. Her breasts shone snowy in the starlight. I went to her; carried her to a couch nearby. My hands felt her skin turning from chill to warm to fiery—

With this highborn woman, love was different from what it had ever been before. There was no thought of proficiency, or of good or bad, right or wrong. Because of her, it was right; it was meant to be; it was *destined*.

Even our very bodies offered us proof. It seemed as if we fit each other perfectly. As if the gods had designed and crafted us to please no partners but each other. We shared a joyous moment—no, many long and increasingly ardent moments—and then we shared a final ecstasy I suspect only the gods and a few rare mortals are ever privileged to know.


A long distance beneath the railing of the terrace, the harbor sea rolled and thundered, reminding us even as we caressed gently in the aftermath that time, implacable time, was rolling inevitably on.

"Julius—" Her lips were gentler than down against my cheek. A moment later, kissing her eyes, I tasted tears. "There is no hope for us, is there?"

"While the war lasts, none." The ecstasy was fading. "The gods have cursed us, I think—"

"Then this night must be enough. Hold me, Julius! Touch me again. There—here—*ohhh*—"

Once more our bodies interlocked, and our hearts beat like the sea far below. Once more, but with even greater intensity than before, she cried out and writhed

182

against me. It was then I knew I would never love any other woman more than I loved her—the woman I could never possess.

As I held her trembling body there on the couch in the inevitable sweet drowsiness following our passion—as I again kissed her shoulder, her throat, every dear part of her—I recollect that something strange happened. I, a hardy and hardened soldier of Rome, felt tears in my own eyes.

Presently we retired to the comfort of the house where we talked sadly on into the night. Each question, each answer, somehow made me realize I should never have come to the villa. Leaving would be all the harder this time.

She asked much about the negotiations. When I had answered most of those questions, she sighed:

"Daily my half-brother grows less tolerant of the young king. Yet for all his inexperience, Hieronymus is a wise ruler. One day, Julius, I'm afraid Hippocrates will take the popularity that he's won with his cheap, inflammatory talk, and turn that popularity against Hieronymus for his own ends. Hippocrates craves the throne—"

"There may be a siege, a battle and a grave for him instead."

"I know your army far outnumbers the one quartered here in the city. But I still hear a great deal of whispering about the engines Archimedes designed a long time ago."

"Do they really exist?"

"I don't honestly know. But at dinner one night last week, Hippocrates grew quite drunk and babbled about them. He claimed he knew where they were stored. In

183

some great, forgotten rooms directly under the palace. Giant catapults and other contraptions, devilish beyond description. Not many of them, he said—just a few prototype models. But if he had those, others could be built."

Her fingers tightened on mine. "Perhaps if your general knew of the threat of the machines, it might promote an armistice instead of a siege—why do you shake your head?"

"It's an ill-founded hope, Cynthia. Marcellus has heard the rumors too. He doesn't believe the engines exist."

"Then let us pray he's right—and that my half-brother was only spouting drunken prattle."

To banish the dismal subject, we made love again. Soon it was morning. A knock sounded. I answered, expecting the little redheaded slut, but finding instead the slave who had presumably drowsed on the front steps all night.

Time had run out.

I threw my cloak around me and bent over Cynthia to kiss her one last time.

"Know this much," I told her. "I can never have you because I'm a common soldier—no, don't speak. Let me finish. But I will never forget what you gave me. Not until the day I die. Remember, always remember that I love you."

"Julius, I love you too, my darling!" She cried then.

I left her.

The slave in the street advised me to hurry. Closing the outer door, I started:

"What was that?"

I pushed the door open again, staring back into the dark antechamber.

"Nothing, master."

"But I heard a sound—"

"Master, please!" the slave protested. "The palace guard changes at dawn. We had best be away or our return will be detected!"

I closed the villa doors. Yet all the way back to the palace, I was increasingly certain my ears hadn't deceived me. I was sure I'd heard a voice like that of the slave girl Daphne, hidden away in the shadows, and laughing—

Laughing softly, perhaps. But laughing.

# CHAPTER XI

# *FALSE WITNESS*

As the seventh day of the truce sessions opened, I was leaning drowsily on my spear when a commotion began at the hall doors:

"Lords! Your indulgence!"

I jerked my head around. The speaker was Kyron. Until then, I hadn't noticed he was missing, so tedious had the meetings become. Kyron rushed to Hippocrates, whispered briefly, then presented himself before Hieronymus. This time he paused, searching the circle of Greek and Roman guards stationed alternately around the hall until he located me.

The moment he spotted me, he said in a loud voice, "Your Excellency, for the past three days I have been investigating a most delicate matter. I now believe it must be brought to your attention, so that the sham of these negotiations will not continue. The Romans have used this parley—undertaken in good faith on our part—as a screen for sending agents abroad to spy on and subvert our people."

Pulvius's wrecked face twisted as he leaped up:

"Be careful, my friend! That's a serious charge."

All around the walls, Greek and Roman hands tensed on their spears.

"But it is a charge for which we have ample proof," Kyron retorted. He spun and shouted, "Bring her in!"

On the great staircase, three armored soldiers appeared pushing a woman before them. Her fine linen gown was now stained with prison filth. Her hair was disarrayed. Even though she was plainly frightened, she did her best to walk with an air of calm, and proud defiance. The hand around my spear turned white, I was clutching it so hard. The other hand dropped toward my sword hilt. The woman the soldiers manhandled down the stairs to face Hippocrates and the young king was Cynthia.

"On the first evening of these negotiations," Kyron announced, "one of the Roman soldiers attached to the negotiating party conferred with this fine lady over matters pertaining to the defense of Greek territory. And the spy—" Kyron did not need the glance around; I knew he was directing his words at me. "—the spy is in this chamber. He will shortly be identified."

I held the spear more tightly. Pulvius showed genuine alarm—a very rare thing for him. He knew, as I did, that because we were outnumbered in the center of enemy city, we must make no rash moves.

I caught Cynthia glancing at me. Her violet eyes seemed to be laboring to give me some explanation. I turned away, deliberately. *No matter what happens,* I thought, *I must make no move until it's too late for anything but desperation—and force.* I only wondered how long I could contain my fear and my rage.

Young Hieronymus was on his feet, pettishly saying to Pulvius, "But if the charge is true, you have indeed abused our courtesy and mocked our trust—"

"Your Highness," Kyron cried, "it is proved beyond a doubt! A witness has come forward."

And as if on signal, another woman appeared in the high doorway where I had first seen Cynthia. This one's hair glowed like fire. Kyron extended his right hand, gesturing for her to come forward without fear. Daphne minced along, playing at being awed. The slave girl prostrated herself before Hieronymus's throne chair.

"Rise, girl," Kyron said. "You have nothing to fear from our monarch."

"He will see to it," Hippocrates put in, "that the malefactors, not you, are the ones punished."

Slowly Daphne stood up. But her head remained bowed.

Kyron asked then, "You are a servant girl employed by this lady who is temporarily occupying a villa on the sea wall?" The rotten stink of the plot was becoming more apparent every moment. Kyron was quite careful not to mention the name of the Greek savant who owned the villa.

"I am, sir," Daphne answered in a sickeningly meek voice.

"Kindly tell us what you saw and overheard there one evening recently."

"This woman—" Daphne did not dare meet Cynthia's eyes. "—this woman, a Greek citizen, has been my mistress for two years. But I would give my life to be free of serving her, and I say that for one simple reason. She has betrayed her countrymen. She entertained a Roman soldier. They talked about the defenses. She told him all she knew. Told him in great detail—"

Hatred of the treacherous, jealous little whore nearly drove me forward to gut her with my spear. Daphne began to sob in a splendid imitation of confusion. Kyron threw an arm across her shoulder. Hippocrates looked strangely expectant, Hieronymus uncertain, Pulvius dismayed. I noticed Pulvius begin to glance around the hall; counting spears; gauging chances for escape.

"This public-spirited girl is obviously upset," Kyron purred. "There is no need to trouble this patriotic girl any further just now. Prior to her coming here, I've taken her testimony in detail, on tablets which I will be happy to place at your disposal. I only brought her into this hall to establish the charges, against our Roman friends—" His eyes glowed, venomous. "And against the traitorous Lady Cynthia."

Hippocrates shook his head. "In the face of treason. I can no longer claim her as my relative. For her the penalty must be a public whipping at very least—"

"I have no taste for such treatment of women," Hieronymus hedged.

"But this is a case of treason!" Hippocrates thundered.

"She is your own kinswoman!"

"I tell you that makes no difference." Hippocrates glared at his half-sister. "None!"

"The lash will help her repent the error of her ways," Kyron added with a smirk.

Hieronymus raised a hand. "But she must at least be permitted to speak in her own defense—"

Dread weighed on me at that moment. I heard Cynthia give the answer I feared. "No. I will not dignify such a patently ridiculous charge by answering."

"Guilty, obviously guilty!" Kyron cried.

"Aye," Hippocrates said. "The witness establishes it, and so does public gossip. Even I have heard of Lady Cynthia's infatuation with a Roman soldier who assisted her after an accident on a Lentini road—"

His scarred face turned white, Pulvius intervened; rose and raised his arms for attention:

"My lords! If there is treachery here, be assured it is not the doing of those of us in charge of the delegation. We are ignoring the real culprit—the soldier in question. Let us find him. I will personally see to it that he suffers for—"

"No, the woman!" Kyron shouted him down. *"The woman first!"*

His jealousy could no longer be contained. From a nearby Greek guard he snatched a long lash, uncoiled it and held it forward to the young king. "Order the first stroke laid on, Your Excellency!"

Hieronymus looked increasingly unsure of him. "But the facts in this matter are still not fully established or documented. We must avoid rash—"

"I'm sick of this vacillating!" Hippocrates roared, storming forward and kicking a stool out of his way. He snatched the whip from Kyron, spun Cynthia around and thrust her into the arms of two Greek slaves. "If we're to be worthy of being called men, we must act like men! Punish the Roman, yes. But the betrayer who is one of our own must be punished first. I repeat, my lords—although she is my own kinswoman, I have long suspected her of harboring unpatriotic ideas." A last, withering glare at Hieronymus. "And I,

191

at least, am man enough to see that she gets what's due her."

And with a rough hand, he ripped Cynthia's gown.

The rip exposed her flesh from her shoulders to the gentle swell of her buttocks. Her humiliation was heartbreaking to behold. A red tide was beating in my head now—

"Let this be a lesson to Syracuse and its king," Hippocrates spat. "Even her own kinsman will not see her go unpunished!"

The lash coiled and cracked. Cynthia screamed. I saw blood trickle down between her shoulders. Then my spear was back over my shoulder, its bronze haft aimed at Hippocrates' chest. I hurled it straight at him.

# CHAPTER XII

# DEATH FOR THE KING

*"Get control of yourself, you damned fool!"*

The shouting of Pulvius was muffled by the ferocious clang of the spear striking the marble floor a hand's width from where Hippocrates stood with a red lash trailing from his fist.

The Greeks on my left and right pulled their swords. Pulvius was still shouting, but I could make no sense of his cries because of the thud of running feet. More Greek men-at-arms spilled into the hall, weapons drawn. Out of nowhere, the blade of the Greek guard on my left slashed at my throat—

I was a fraction slow to pull my own sword. I wrenched back to avoid the killing thrust, then chopped down at the Greek's wrists. Metal hit bone. The guard screamed and tried to dodge away—too late. The guard on my right was charging. The sword of the second Greek stuck the first man straight through the belly. And then chaos descended on the hall.

Realizing the immense danger of the situation, Pulvius limped for the entrance opposite the one through which fresh squads of slaves and soldiers were pouring. *"Out this way!"* Pulvius howled, raising his sword as a rallying sign. "All together, or we'll never get out alive—" Then three Greeks attacked him.

Back to back, Pulvius and another Roman soldier fought them off. Two more pounced on me, alternately slamming their round shields at my head and cutting at me with their swords. I dodged, chopping the exposed tendons at the back of the leg of one of them. He wailed and reeled away. The other came darting in. From my half-crouched position I stabbed for his stomach. He shrieked in agony, then pitched over.

I had a moment to glance at the hall. With sick horror, I saw that Cynthia had vanished, probably spirited away by Kyron. Here and there groups of two or three from the Roman guard faced far larger numbers, all fighting desperately.

Again I searched for some sign of Cynthia in the confusion. But she was definitely gone. I raced to join Pulvius.

Slaves from the far side of the hall were casting spears. A Greek captain screamed at them to be careful. One of the last shafts caught Daphne squarely between the breasts as she tried to flee. I watched her eyes glazing.

Pulvius and his Roman guard were getting the better of the four or five men harrying them; the Greeks were not heavily armored. I rammed my blade into the spine of one of the enemy. His strangled shriek rang out.

Then, between the bobbing heads of members of our party struggling to rally around Pulvius, I saw the young ruler Hieronymus topple forward. He sprawled on marble with a short sword planted between his shoulder blades. I had a quick, distorted impression of a man stepping away, his hands empty—

Hippocrates.

Pulvius shouted, *"Don't wait for the rest!* Run for your lives—and use steel on anyone who tries to stop you!"

Leading the way, he charged out of the hall and down a long corridor stretching into the distance. Two dozen of us, many wounded and bleeding, loped at his heels. Only as we ran did I begin to comprehend what I had just seen—Hippocrates seizing the moment to assure his power. As we ran through the darkened halls, meeting only a few unarmed servants who hung back, halloos and alarms dwindled away behind us. Astonished, I realized we were not being actively pursued. We were being given a chance to escape because we had inadvertently helped to give Hippocrates what he wanted—

An empty throne.

I thought I discerned the pattern of the plot then. Out of jealousy, Daphne had gone to the general, or to Kyron or some lesser underling. From her information had been fashioned a trumped-up confrontation that would provoke a battle in the hall. In the heat of that battle Hippocrates might have a chance to strike down the king, and it had happened as he'd hoped. What enraged me most was his callous use of his own half-sister in the scheme.

Tormented by worry over what had become of her, and at the same time knowing it would be insanity to venture off searching for her in a palace whose layout I did not know well, I could only hope that since she had fulfilled her part in the plan, Hippocrates would not deal harshly with her.

"Our luck is proving too good," Pulvius panted as we sped through sunlit yards toward the stables where we had quartered our horses. "Suspiciously good. Well, let's not question it. Mount up, ride for the gates and don't stop to answer to anyone. The king's death must have thrown things into total confusion—"

Or, Hippocrates never meant to pursue at all, I thought stumbling on, my lungs aching from the effort of running. *Murder* was quite enough to satisfy him today.

I grew increasingly sure of that as we took to our horses and galloped away, unmolested.

When we reached the garrison camp, we found a feverish state of activity. Everywhere the legions were drilling. Siege towers were being erected on their great round wheels. I soon learned that the last flotilla of ninety huge warships had reached anchorage just off the beach below our camp. Engineers were already rigging the ships for the attack on Syracuse, which was to begin in a matter of days now that negotiations had collapsed.

For three sleepless nights I fretted over Cynthia's fate while I listened to the hammers of the engineers and the blowing of trumpets. Galleys and triremes were being chained together in units of three, forming huge monster-vessels. On the center deck of each, a great square wooden fighting tower was raised. Those towers, I realized, would reach to the top of the sea wall of Syracuse when the ships were in the water directly below. From the towers, men could pour across boarding planks into the city, lending support to the land forces.

On the third day I again felt compelled to seek an audience with Marcellus. The general kept me waiting three hours, and when I was at last ushered in, he greeted me curtly:

"Once more I meet you in unhappy circumstances, Prefect. The riot—the whipping of the woman—Hieronymus dead and the chance for peace lost—" Dourly he shook his head.

Then he sighed and laid his hand on wax-covered tablets. "Pulvius saved me a report of the whole dubious affair. The same wench as before, eh—?"

"Yes, sir. I'm sure she's on our side."

"Is she, now!" He tapped his field desk, clearly skeptical. "Well. What of it? Why are you here? Did she give you more so-called secret information?"

"Again, none I can prove, General—" I wanted to remind him that Cynthia's earlier warnings about Hippocrates had turned out to be accurate, but thought it prudent not to irritate him any further. Conveying what I had to say was more important:

"But it bears repeating." In brief sentences, I told him about the siege engines Cynthia had mentioned. "She admitted Hippocrates was drunk when he referred to them. But why would even a drunken man boast about such things—especially with no Romans present—if he knew they didn't exist?"

"I can't say," Marcellus shrugged. "I'm not going to waste time wondering, however. I have more practical matters to deal with—and I refuse to bother my staff with speculations about an old stargazer's fairy-tale devices."

197

"Sir, Cynthia swore Hippocrates knew where they are stored this very moment."

*"Enough!"* he exclaimed. "The siege will go forward—without concern for mythical machines! Perhaps the collapse of the peace parley will turn out to be a blessing. The spies report the city's in a turmoil. With the young king dead, slain not by a Roman but by a Greek, I hope to find a great many citizens ready to aid us. I'm counting on a decisive win—and a relatively quick one."

I was not convinced, but I held my tongue.

He fixed me with a thoughtful stare. "Yes, things are working out almost as I planned. Of course I was surprised when Hippocrates used the parley to arrange an assassination. Your dalliance with the woman proved a convenient pretext, but I'm sure he'd have found another if you hadn't proved so extremely helpful."

His mockery rankled. "Sir—" I began.

"Never mind, never mind!" he said, something sly creeping into his expression. "You were right about Hippocrates, and that I acknowledge. But he isn't the only one who can turn circumstances to his advantage. I myself used the parley as a screen. A concealment. I never expected the negotiations to amount to anything, although I told no one—Pulvius included. When he learned that after he returned, it rankled him. Still, my purpose was served. The parley helped cover the delay until the last war galleys arrived."

"You mean you sent us into Syracuse with no intention of accepting a peace treaty, General?"

"No intention," he repeated. "That is why I would not presume to hold you responsible for anything that happened. There is only one answer to these Greeks—force. Because of your ridiculous entangle-

198

ments with that woman, in your own blundering way you've helped me deliver that answer—"

He rose. "But I still remember the distasteful incident with your tribune friend. I'm frankly weary of you, Prefect. Take care you give me no cause to summon you again. When I hear your name next time, let it be in connection with some valorious deed in battle and with nothing else. *Dismissed!*"

Hurt by his scorn, I stumbled out. How clever was he after all, I wondered. *Were* the engines of Archimedes only fancies? Legends?

Soon I had no time for further speculation. I went down the cliffs with hundreds of others, once again a foot soldier because of a temporary reorganization for the massive assault on the port. I went aboard one of those peculiar three-hulled vessels and took my place near the scaling tower on the center deck. I was afraid for the success of the whole venture.

But trumpets were blowing on the bluff. The land forces marched out, commanded by Appius. It was too late for any one man to stop the Roman war machine from rolling.

# CHAPTER XIII

# SEA DOOM

Wind bellied the great sails on the two outer ships of our three-hulled craft. We glided peacefully, moving fast. The rising sun cast a scarlet sheen across the lapping water and burnished the armor of the men crouched beside me on deck, their faces pale.

The leading galleys, six three-hullers out of a total of eighteen, soon drew near the bluff and the wall above. Speaking trumpets amplified commands from helmsman to helmsman. With much creaking of gear and flapping of canvas, the six towering ships began to swing to port in unison to form a line prow-to-stern. After our six disgorged their men through their towers, six more would slip in, then another six.

"Something's wrong," a tribune muttered, gazing up at the walls of Syracuse. "The silence is too perfect. I'm not used to this kind of silence before an attack.

It's as if no one's there—no one's waiting for us." He swabbed perspiration from his cheek.

"I agree," I said. "The Greek watchmen certainly must have seen us when we rounded the headland—"

Again the tribune nervously studied the ramparts, against which the black shadows of the towers now fell. "They saw us," he whispered. "I heard their bugles myself, and glimpsed some heads. Since then, though, those walkways on top have been empty."

"Perhaps Appius is keeping them busy on the land side," someone else suggested.

The tribune made a ritual sign against the evil eye. "If so, I pray that the wind changes so we can catch the sound of his horns and know that he is—*wait*! Did I hear something?"

A leadsman was softly chanting the water depth as the sun brightened. He was quickly hushed. Hundreds of pairs of eyes searched the black, forbidding city wall under which the six ships bobbed, positioned in line. I had heard that sound myself: a faint grinding or wrenching, as though unseen siege engines were in operation.

No other noise reached us. The wind was blowing the wrong way. Where did the clanking come from? It was as if our fleet had sailed into a harbor of ghosts, and we were to attack a citadel of the dead—

"On the headland!" a soldier cried suddenly. "Look—the signal!"

The tribune was so overwrought, he struck the man in the face. *"Be silent!"* But relief showed on his leathery features moments later. We knew what the column of smoke signified. Wet wood had been lighted to inform the fleet that Appius had launched his assault on the land walls with catapults and scaling ladders.

The smoke boiled into the calm, shell-pink sky. All across the harbor, silver bugles rang from one galley to another. The tribune stepped back from the dark entrance to the high tower:

"Inside! Go up three abreast! Scream and yell and let them know that you are coming—and can't be stopped!"

I was in the sixth rank. I was fastening my helmet when I heard two other distinct sounds. The first was a rattling of the planks run out at the top of the tower to touch the ramparts. The second, kin to the strange noise of a few moments earlier, was a clanking and rattling of a great chain.

If I hadn't been jostled by anxious men behind me, I would not have dropped my sword. Nor would I have still been on deck when the new shadow fell across us in the reddish morning light.

To a man, those of us ready to enter the tower jerked our heads up. As in some fatal death-dream, an unbelievable *claw* came gliding into space over the top of the wall.

Such a claw had never been seen before on earth. From prong to curved prong, it was roughly ten times as wide as a man was tall. Elsewhere along the wall, similar claws began to appear. All the claws were gray iron, dully reflecting the red sun.

At last the clanking made sense. Giant crane devices from which hung link chains swung the claws out over the harbor wall. A soldier behind me retched. Another fainted. The various captains at the helms of the great vessels began shouting to each other in dismay with their speaking trumpets. Loudest of all sounded the massed bugles on Marcellus's bridge, still signalling the attack.

Ten prongs to a claw, eight of the claws dropped through space toward the ships below. The clank of unreeling chain filled the air. Then, in those startled seconds there arose from the battlements of Syracuse a scream of fury and triumph from what sounded like a hundred thousand Greek throats.

All at once scores of heads appeared on the ramparts. The air was suddenly filled with a rain of arrows and metal bolts, firepots and stones. Cynthia's warning had been right.

The machines of Archimedes were real.

*"Back off—back off!"* Our helmsman was shrieking. Pandemonium had spread across the deck. Tribunes were bawling orders for us to start up through the towers. We obeyed, though before I got inside the hot, sweaty-smelling dark, three of the men in line with me had died. One took an arrow in his throat. Two others were killed by falling rocks.

*"Go back! Go down! The cranes—"*

Wild cries drifted from the men already on the ladders overhead. At the tower's top, a claw appeared, dropping, dropping while it swung from side to side.

Amid rising yells of anguish and the crackle of fires started in our rigging by the firepots, there was a heavier crash. The swinging claw sheared off the top of the scaling tower.

There are scarcely words to describe the horror of watching the top section of the tower sail out through space with peculiar, almost unbearable slowness, bodies tumbling out of it from all sides. A dozen men were smashed to pulp against the cliff. Their blood ran down among the white limestone streaks. Other men fell on top of me, plummeting from the shattered ladders. We had been comrades before, but now we were maddened animals, struggling with each other, clawing to get free so we could fight—

But there was nothing to fight except falling fire and rock, and those great claws coming down, steadily down—

The prow of the triple vessel ahead of ours lifted into the air like a bird taking flight. A claw-machine had closed over the vessel's ramming beak. As though the ship were a toy, the chain and claw pulled that incredibly heavy triple craft out of the water until its decks were sharply aslant.

Screaming men slipped off into the sea. All along the line of ships, other prows were jerked upward. How the Greeks managed to clamp the claws on with such devilish accuracy, I did not know. But in a matter of moments, those fiendish engines had carried the day.

The deck lurched beneath me. I slid into a mast and clung tight. Another wrench; our prow lifted again. Three soldiers went scrambling hysterically up the deck, out of their wits. They reached the rail and foolishly began hacking at the monster prongs clamped there.

"Over the side!" an officer shouted. "Into the water and swim for your lives!"

The whole world reeled as the claw gave another pull.

I lost my grip on the mast and went skidding down the deck which now hung nearly perpendicular in space. Bodies fell by—a confusion of screaming faces, pieces of armor, men clutching one another. Then there was nothing below me but a flash of blood-reddened water.

Frantically I threw away my sword. Tore off my helmet. I struck, landing on another man a second after the claw released our prow and the triple huller had smashed down again. Everywhere, men were yelling:

"A Roman, a Roman—throw a line, here is a Roman!"

Paddling and trying to keep my sanity in that devil's sea, I realized the men were appealing to legionnaries who lined the rails of the galleys that had not quite come within range of the claws. Kicking off my greaves, I swam toward the hazy line of those ships. The triple-hullers were retreating; whoever did not catch a lifeline now would be left behind to drown.

No, not drown, I realized dully as my arms grew heavier and the distance to the nearest ropes trailing in the water seemed half a world away. Above the clank of the claw-chains being retracted now that the flotilla had begun to sail off, new, sharp cries were ringing out. From small black ports hewn into the cliff wall, Greek skiffs put out, manned by soldiers who dragged all survivors aboard as prisoners.

The water seemed to crawl with hundreds of these little vessels. Frenzied orders were bawled on the Roman galleys as their captains cracked whips and drove soldiers to the auxiliary oars. One galley remained close enough for me to catch. Men were already scrambling up wet lines to the safety of its rail. But the strength of my arms was failing. I was barely able to turn my head in order to draw breath as I swam.

The hail of rocks and crossbow darts from the high walls had slacked off now that the skiffs were in open water. Only the knowledge of what might befall me kept me swimming. To a soldier, being a prisoner was worse—far worse—than dying.

Only a few more ropes hung from the rail of the galley. One or two men were poised with coils, looking for the last likely candidates for survival. I raised my arm.

"A Roman," I cried feebly. "Throw a line here!"

The wake of the galley began to wash over me, floods of bloody foam smashing across my face, into my eyes, between my lips. I thought my lungs would break open when I shouted again:

*"A Roman! Throw a line!"*

A splendidly armored soldier half hidden in smoke pointed to me. Desperately, I flung both hands over my head, waving. The gods be praised!—he saw me!

The soldier lifted the weight at the end of his line, and swung it several times to get momentum. But his cast fell short. I could not begin to reach it. Didn't that man have any strength? Didn't he have an eye to judge his distance?

The line was hauled back toward the galley which was rapidly pulling out of range. The man would not be able to try again—

And then I saw he had missed for good reason.

The smoke had thinned. I saw him clearly as he leaned on a rail of what the pennons identified as Marcellus's flagship. There was amusement on the scarred face of Sardus Pulvius.

The galley's stern was growing smaller and smaller. He had known who I was. He had cast short on purpose. The final trick had fallen to him after all.

"Here's a squirming fish!" came a shout in Greek.

I twisted around to look, nearly smashed in the skull by the prow of a skiff. Swarthy faces bent toward me. I struck at the hands; cursed; cried a name. Their laughter rang as they caught hold of me.

"Another Roman—clean out of his head. Come aboard, soldier! Sorry there's no lady named Cynthia to welcome you. You'll have to be satisfied with us men of General Hippocrates—"

I lay sprawled and gagging in the reeking bilge on the bottom of the skiff. One of the men kicked my temple. I rolled over, and dimly heard the Roman ship trumpets sound full retreat. Overhead the sun changed to Cynthia's face, then to a round and burning shackle—a sign of the slavery that awaited me. The slavery or even something worse—

In a flare of pain and white fire, even that sun soon went dark.

# Part Three

# THE
# INFERNAL MACHINES

# CHAPTER I

# ON THE RAMPARTS

For a week, as nearly as I could reckon, I was kept with other Roman soldiers in the filth and darkness of a dungeon beneath the military headquarters in Syracuse. By the end of that time, the weakest had died.

Some went silently. Some cried in pain, or wept, as rats ran over their limbs in the fetid dark. Those of us who survived on the maggoty bread and slops, delivered once a day, were finally herded out. We were lined up beside a forge in the yard. There a smith fastened a thick chain to the left ankle of every man. From this prisoner's bracelet hung a small metal disk inscribed with some Greek characters. I presumed the disk identified the wearer as a slave.

Next we were divided into groups of several dozen each and marched from the central quarter, through the inner walls to the outer ones. Blinking and stumbling in the sunlight, and half dead from hunger, I saw the giant engine which was to become my companion.

Timber uprights supported huge platforms jutting from the inner face of the high wall. Ladders led up to these platforms. We climbed slowly while the overseer's whip cracked at our heels. On the platform—mine was only one of many to my right and left—there stood a catapult.

A catapult more suitable to gods than men, I thought blearily. The base was twice my height. The firing rope was as thick around as a man's arm. Another smith waited at the machine, leather-aproned and grinning. I saw chains laid out, one end of each already fastened to the machine's base by great iron staples.

The fifty of us assigned to this engine were split into two files. One group went to either side of the base. The smith affixed a ring to the free end of each chain, then closed a ring around each man's arm. My ring was placed on the left side. Thus I became a working part of Archimedes's infernal creation.

Six times that morning we discharged the great catapult. Each operation took a while. But there were six other engine platforms close by. Consequently one machine was usually in the process of firing.

That day the Roman assault was brief and unsuccessful. When it was over we had nothing to do but sink down beside the base of the catapult and wait, exhausted and heartsick, until the next call to battle.

How many weeks passed on the platform, I am not sure. I was feverish a good deal of the time because of exposure to the scorching sun and the cool night air. My body ached constantly. Pulling the firing rope was

212

terrible work. On the average of twice a day the overseer would call us to our stations. After a while, though, the Roman assaults occurred less frequently.

Something in me clung foolishly to life, even though it seemed that such effort was futile. In one twilight hour, two men I remembered all too well appeared on the ramparts overhead. To my dismay, I saw they intended to climb down the ladder to our platform, doubtless on a tour of the fortifications. I huddled against the base of the catapult, hoping my beard would hide my features.

"—on closer inspection, worthy Damippus," said Hippocrates who was standing just a few steps away, "you'll observe there is no magic in our great machines, only clever engineering."

With the general and his companion, was Kyron, looking red-eyed and slightly tipsy. Feigning slumber, I watched them through slitted eyes. Hatred would not let me turn away completely, even though I knew that if they recognized me, I would probably be killed outright.

The member of the party addressed as Damippus wore a tunic and robe of a peculiar foreign cut. Large gold pendants hung from his pierced ears. He shielded his eyes from the sinking sun and gazed up at the catapult's firing cup.

"Very impressive, my lords. Taking these beauties into consideration, I'm sure the council at Sparta will look favorably on my report of this visit—and the recommendations the report will contain."

Kyron smiled. "We trust so, Damippus. These Roman prisoners won't live forever, you know. And the siege promises to be a long one. We will need reinforcements. It's ironic, but scores of humans are required to make one god in the machine."

Damippus smiled at the witticism. "Be assured I'll ask the council at Sparta to issue an immediate request for volunteers to sail here to aid you. My galley will leave on the night tide tomorrow. As soon as I rendezvous with the important personage I mentioned earlier—" Here Damippus gave them a significant look, as though wary of saying too much. "—I will be bound home for Sparta."

Hippocrates seized his visitor's arm. "When you keep your rendezvous, be sure you describe our faithful stewardship of his cause."

The Spartan nodded briskly. "Oh, believe me, I shall! When I presented my credentials in Latium and told of my intentions to sail here secretly for a personal inspection, I was specifically asked to report on how you were faring. Without Syracuse as a port, our mutual friend is virtually helpless. Cut off from supplies. That's why I'm to be met at sea. Before continuing on to Sparta, I'll deliver a firsthand account of your—"

*"Hold!"* Kyron's voice cut sharply through the darkening air. "That's enough talk for the moment."

Hippocrates frowned, puzzled. Kyron whispered to the general. I huddled against the machine's base, my face fully averted. Kyron's gaze had flickered across mine, moved on, then jerked back again. I heard the thud of his boots as he strode forward. Then I heard his slurred voice:

"Gentlemen, it appears we may have chosen the wrong platform to inspect. I fear someone's been paying close attention to our discussion—"

214

Standing over me, he caught hold of my hair and dragged me to my feet. His eyes flew wide in astonishment.

"Overseer!" he shouted. *"Overseer—your sword!"*

But the overseer had disappeared for the moment.

"Who is it?" Hippocrates asked. "Just some dirty— in the name of Artemis, *no!* You have sharper eyes than I, Kyron."

Kyron smiled in a bleary way. "Could anyone forget him? Not I, certainly."

"Nor could I forget you, whoreson," I said, no longer caring about what happened.

Kyron prepared to strike me with his hand. Abruptly, Hippocrates laid a ringed hand on his arm:

"Softly! The rest of these fools are dozing—"

"Yes," Kyron agreed. "But this one knows Greek. The others don't."

Damippus, the Spartan, blinked in a confused way.

Hippocrates said to him, "My lord, I fear that we've discoursed too freely here. We assumed we were safe. That was a mistake. We know this fellow. A Roman soldier. Obviously captured during the first assault. And while it's doubtful that he heard all we said, or that he could release himself from the embraces of his lady love—" The general touched my coiled armchain. "—we must take every precaution." He smiled coldly at me. "If we'd known you'd been captured, Roman, we would have attended to you sooner—"

Old jealousy burned in Kyron's arrogant eyes. "It would be practical, General, to make certain he can say nothing about our distinguished secret visitor—"

At that moment, the overseer arrived, badly out of breath:

"I'm sorry to delay, my lords. The Romans are in the field again, rolling all their towers and engines forward." That was quickly proved; overhead, shouting men began racing along the ramparts. The sky soon took on a scarlet glare.

"A fire attack, I fear," the overseer went on. "I beg you, my lords, retreat from here."

"Certainly. Only lend me your sword a moment," Hippocrates replied. "And hold this bearded scum so he doesn't struggle."

The overseer cast anxious glances at the heavens. But he was a well-trained man, and he obeyed. Around me, the other slaves were beginning to stir. The overseer grabbed my shoulders from behind. Hippocrates slipped in close, seizing my throat. In truth my strength was so drained by sickness and by the days and nights on the open platform, I could struggle only feebly.

"These precautions may not be necessary," Hippocrates whispered. "But there is personal satisfaction in them as you might guess, eh? *Hold him, overseer!* First we'll blind the eyes. When he yells, we'll cut out his tongue and pierce his eardrums. In that way his silence—his *full* silence—will be assured."

"I beg you, my lords—hurry!" the overseer cried. War trumpets were blaring both inside and outside the walls. The reddish glare brightened steadily. Hippocrates drew his arms back, the sword shimmering. Then, with a hiss and a trail of sparks, a firepot arched over the ramparts.

Instantly, the twilight glared with scores more sailing into sight, all trailing banners of sparks and scarlet flame.

216

"Take cover!" the overseer shrieked, releasing me. The first fireball was hurtling down directly above us.

With a cry of frustration, Hippocrates turned and rammed the sword at my eyes.

# CHAPTER II

# ORDEAL BY FIRE

I lunged away, as far from him as the chain would allow. Hippocrates stumbled as Damippus blundered into him. The tip of Hippocrates' blade buried in the wood base of the catapult. The Spartan was already on his way down the ladder to safety.

The fireball struck the far side of the platform. Kyron shrieked, losing his balance and nearly pitching into space before he regained it. *"A hit, a hit!"* the terrified overseer bellowed.

Flames swirled up, quickly engulfing the platform. Already men in chains were dying on the far side. A charred smell of human flesh floated in the air.

The Greeks melted away like ghosts; their own skins were more important than mine at the moment. The overseer ran wildly to and fro, calling for bucket men to come up from below. More and more hissing fire-pots turned the dusk into blazing day—

Soon half the support timbers of the platform were afire. Hippocrates disappeared down the ladder, followed by Kyron. On either side of me, chained prisoners went berserk. They tugged desperately at the staple-fastened chains, pleading—screaming—to be released.

The catapult's base began to burn, then the platform itself. Gusts of hot smoke fanned over me as I hauled and tugged on my own chain. But the wood around the staple was still intact.

One truth cried out loudly in my frightened mind: if the bucket men rushing up the ladders with their leather pots of water succeeded in quenching the fire, the Greek general and his aide would be back to find me. If I didn't perish in the conflagration, I would certainly perish soon after—

Clouds of steam billowed as the bucket men attacked the flames. But their water supply was too scanty to do much good. The wall of fire was halfway across the platform and sweeping upward, burning the braces of the catapult arm.

My skin began to hurt from the scorching heat. The prisoners on either side of me clashed their chains and screamed like demented men. Desperately, I dropped to one knee and crawled backward, extending my chain to its full. I waited and even prayed a little as the wood on my side of the catapult base smoked, smoldered and then burst alight.

The heat was cruel. But I wanted that fire to grow intense. If the staple didn't heat sufficiently, I wouldn't be able to pull free—

Back and forth like squealing rats, the other chained

220

prisoners ran without plan or purpose. The bucket men had given up and retreated. Even the overseer was hurrying to the ladder now—

Shouts rang from the plain outside the city. Here and there roofs in Syracuse were burning. The flames crept nearer to the line of chain staples. I watched my staple begin to glow cherry-red, shouting to a petrified boy near me:

"Don't struggle! Wait for the proper moment, then tug it loose!"

But fear was riding him; fear determined all his responses. He made a wild lunge for the edge of the platform, tangling himself in his chain. Suddenly, overhead, one of the uprights crumbled and fell on him. He shrieked and disappeared beneath the fiery wreckage.

I choked in the smoke, my face felt as though the heat would soon broil my skin away. But the iron of my staple was growing brighter and brighter—

Then the platform itself began to sway. The night became a bedlam of screaming, and the creak of engines on the other, unhit platforms. Sweat poured off my forehead, nearly blinding me. The wood all around the staple was afire. Heat was creeping along the chain itself, searing my palms as I grasped it in both hands. With the last strength left to me, I pulled—

Like some fiery bird surging out of the bright pit of hell, the flowing staple loosened all at once, and came flying at me. The staple and a part of the chain struck me in the chest. The super-heated metal made me shriek with agony.

Somehow I stumbled away, staggering and kicking my way through a writhing mass of prisoners, all of whom were terrified to do anything about their plight.

"Pull on your chains. *Pull them!*" I yelled. "They'll come free if you tug hard enough!"

Down from above crashed another section of the engine, killing a dozen in a shower of fire. The platform supports began to buckle. The scorching wood beneath my naked soles flayed my skin. I saw the escape ladder teeter and start to fall away from the platform's edge. I realized I could save none of the others, for they were too terrified to try to save themselves. I caught the ladder and started to climb down, using just my right hand. In my left I carried the heavy chain, which was mercifully cooling a little.

I was two-thirds of the way down when the ladder lurched again. Above, the entire platform sheared away from the wall. The night filled with trailing banners of fire as I tumbled into space.

I crashed to the earth, stunned and in great pain. For several moments I could not rise. Above me, a river of molten red seemed to be falling—in another instant I'd be buried under the remains of the platform.

Somehow I managed to rise and run, stumbling away as the bodies of men—my comrades still chained—fell, to be crushed or burned to death in the midst of a roar of splintering, flaming wood. A few faint moans rose from the carnage. But no one crawled out alive.

I staggered toward a dark street on the far side of the avenue, praying to the gods that no one would stop me. Carrying the chain, I was too weak to fight.

A Greek horse troop galloped by. A brigade of bucket men ran the other way. My ears hurt from the noise. I came across the overseer lying dead, eyes open. I paused long enough to strip his corpse of his cloak, which I wrapped around my left arm to conceal the chain. Then I plunged into the dark street, and ran for my life.

It seemed that I ran for hours. It cannot have been that long, certainly. By degrees, I came to my senses. I knew I had only one possible haven in all of the city—the villa of Archimedes. So I staggered in the direction of the sea wall—or at least in the direction in which I thought it lay. I was half dead but still unwilling to stop and risk capture.

At an intersection, I slipped in a slime of garbage; fell. The cloak came loose from my arm. The chain snaked out with a hideous clank.

Lanterns bobbed down a lane to my left. "Who goes yonder? Stop and identify—by the gods, he's dragging a chain!"

Then I was up and running again, lugging the chain while the night watch cried behind me.

# CHAPTER III

# SOLDIER'S SANCTUARY

Slipping, reeling, thrashing against the walls and along narrow passageways, I kept ahead of them for several blocks. The ghostly haloes of their lanterns bobbed relentlessly behind.

Soon, my weakened legs began to shudder with the exertion. I cut around a sharp turning of a back street and, at the next intersection, staggered into an alley which led to the grounds of a fine house. By the back wall I crawled into a sewage ditch and lay on my spine in the pitch dark, only my mouth and nose above the foul-smelling water.

"Down here!" one of the watchmen shouted. Lantern light leaked along the passage I'd taken.

"Perhaps he broke into the house—"

"No, the wall's too high for climbing. Let's take the right-hand turning. He can't be far ahead with the

225

chain. We'll find him. And if we don't someone else will. Other search parties will be on the street soon—"

Moments later, I slopped my way out of the stinking water and leaned against the bricks of the wall, sobbing for breath. The haloed lanterns were gone.

Though I'd escaped the pursuers, utter despair overwhelmed me all at once. I was only one man in a city of thousands of enemies. I wanted to give up; lie down again. Rest my tortured body and my weary mind. Perhaps it was only my soldier's training that prevented it. Within moments, I was moving again—

From the glow in the red sky, I concluded that the land wall lay on my right. Therefore the sea wall must be in the opposite direction. The slimy chain was cold against my belly as I hurried on. A cut across my ribs, gotten when I'd scraped against a building, leaked blood.

Most of the residences in this outer quarter were shuttered and dark. Undoubtedly the inhabitants were cowering inside, waiting for the Roman attack to end. I kept on. After several false turns, I caught the scent of the sea.

Presently, reeling like a drunken man, I emerged into a street which seemed familiar. The burning rooftops were far behind, and they were few in number anyway. The Roman fire-throwing machines had a range far less than those designed by Archimedes.

I pounded on the main doors of his villa—
Silence.

To the left of the doors, the wall of the formal front garden loomed. With one awful exertion, I leaped for the top. The chain clanked loudly as I grasped the rim and threw a leg over. I didn't climb to the other side. I fell.

226

The chain was wrapped around me, and my whole body was in torment as I rolled onto my belly and fainted.

Sometime later, I awoke, convinced I had gone mad.

A green firefly light was dancing in the distance. I blinked several times and gradually realized I was gazing through an open portal into the house. The green gleam became the yellow of a lamp wick through thin, emerald-covered hangings.

As quietly as I could, I crawled to my knees. I held the loose end of the chain in my right hand, ready to strike with it. The house wasn't empty after all; perhaps some frightened slave was hunting for a prowler—

As I slipped toward the hanging, the light seemed to draw nearer. I thought I saw the flickering metal glare of a blade, but I could not be sure. Then I perceived a human form behind the light. I recognized the white tunic, but the gauzy green hangings and my own blurred vision hid all other details.

I raised the end of the chain. A hand pushed the hanging aside. The slave stepped through:

*"Who's there?"*

The chain came down, then I jerked it aside at the last instant, tearing a great gouge from the earth where it struck. It was no slave, but a trembling woman—and I had nearly killed her—

"Are there any others in the house?" I asked, still unable to see her behind the glare of the lamp in her hand.

"Don't come any closer," she whispered. "Whatever you want to steal, take it and go. Just don't touch me—"

227

Then I knew who it was:

"Cynthia!"

She hadn't recognized my voice; it had become an exhausted croak. "Cynthia, raise the lamp. Look at my face."

The lamp bobbed—

"*Julius!*"

She screamed it softly, as though she'd seen a dead man. And I must have looked very much like one, my body soot-blackened, my beard down to my chest, the chain dangling from my arm—

For a time, I lost track of my surroundings. I came to, lying upon a couch in one of the sleeping rooms off the peristyle. Cynthia was putting a cloth to my head.

"Don't try to speak," she whispered. "Not until you've rested a little—"

Gently, she touched the places on my chest where the chain staple had burned. I winced, and almost cried out. She'd already tied linen around my ribs where I had been bleeding.

"Wait a moment," she murmured. "I think we have some medicines that might help the burns—"

Her white gown swirled around her as she left. It took her a good while to return. She wept as she cleansed the charred spots with a stinging sponge from a basin.

"This is the only place in the whole city where I thought I might find sanctuary," I said in a rasping voice. "I had no idea you'd be here—"

She smiled bitterly. "Only through the kindness of Archimedes. Oh, Julius—Julius—I died that morning in the great hall of the palace."

"I, too, watching them whipping you. I thought you'd go to prison, or worse."

228

Fighting back tears, she gave a sorrowful little shrug with one shoulder.

"Very nearly, my darling. Strange that I still call you that even when it's too late—" She brushed at her eyes, continuing after a moment:

"Obviously the scene at the palace was all Kyron's doing. And Daphne's. When she died in the hall and you fled with the Romans, Kyron was forced to withdraw his charges for lack of evidence. My half-brother had matters of more pressing concern. The engines—"

"Oh, I have firsthand knowledge of the engines now. I've been chained to one since the harbor attack failed."

"Is that how you came here? You escaped—?"

"Yes, after nearly being killed by your half-brother and Kyron." As quickly as I could, I told her of my capture, my enforced service on the platform and my flight during the fire attack. At the end I said, "I'm not any too sure we're safe here, either. It's possible some other Romans may have escaped from that engine. I heard the watch say additional search parties would be out soon—"

She glanced at the doorway. "No fugitives could hide anywhere except the outer quarter. They couldn't possibly pass into the central city. They may indeed come searching from house to house, as you say."

Anguish made me grip her hand. "I nearly wish I hadn't found you again."

"Don't say such things! At least we have a moment together."

"I thought Archimedes might be in the house. Perhaps it was foolish, but I hoped he might help me get back to the Roman lines. I *must* get back to them—use my sword again—"

Her sweetly scented palm touched my lips. "Please don't. Your face turns so ugly when you say that—"

"Ugly for an ugly world. Where is the old man?"

"Staying in his rooms at the palace. He wanted me to have the run of the house. And once Hieronymus was dead, Hippocrates truly didn't care whether I was punished or not. My esteemed half-brother had what he wanted. Power. I'm ashamed to admit I was grateful when they let me go. Now I'm doubly grateful, and not the least ashamed—"

And with a soft, lost cry, she pressed her mouth on mine. We kissed long, but with little joy. There was too much pain in meeting again in such confused and hopeless circumstances.

Presently I thrust her away. "Please give me another cup of wine. I must collect my thoughts. Even wearing this—" I rattled the chain attached to the shackle on my left arm. "—perhaps I can find a way back to the legions. But before I put my mind to it, finish telling me why you're here and not in prison."

She rose, brought the wine and then began to pace. Her face showed incredible strain as she spoke:

"This is very nearly like a prison, my darling. As I said, Kyron didn't press charges after Daphne died. Still, the news of my alleged treachery became widespread very soon. Hippocrates did let the matter drop, but not without a token gesture of punishment. They impounded my goods and sealed my house—"

She shuddered, and went on with some effort: "I was turned out to shift for myself. Only Archimedes showed any kindness at all. He offered to let me stay here since the house is empty."

"Where are his slaves?"

"Gone off to the ramparts to fight. I've lived here

230

several weeks now. Only one thing's kept me alive." Her violet eyes looked deep into mine. "The memory of you."

I made my way slowly to the doorway, gazing out through the darkened peristyle. "Well, it's a fine lover you chose. A Roman prisoner with a chain on him. Come, let's walk in the air—I need to decide what I'm going to do."

Just then a new thought intruded. Might there not be a way out of this accursed city for her as well? Even feeling as I did—that the very idea was impossible—I couldn't stop thinking about it.

She took my arm and went with me to the terrace, a wind-swept place strangely calm even with the firelight in the heavens. Far below, I heard the purling of the waves in the harbor. We stood at the balustrade, gazing down. On the curved shore of the bay opposite us, torches burned.

"The legions in the field," I said, half-aloud. "Just across there. It might as well be another world."

"Are they attacking tonight, Julius?"

"Probably. They've been attacking for weeks, but it's wasted effort. The old man's engines are too powerful."

Cynthia gripped the rail and stared at the panorama of the siege camp across the black water. "I know my own people would again curse me for a traitor for saying it. But tonight, I—I do wish the Romans were in the streets, and in power. Hippocrates grows vainer and more arrogant every day. He doesn't care how many lives are lost defending the city. He doesn't care a whit for the cause of Carthage, either. All he cares about is having power and using it."

The wind whispered in the silence. I shrugged. "Perhaps it will all end soon. There's no hope of a Roman victory with those machines guarding the walls."

I heard her gasp softly, then begin to tap her hand on the rail. "Julius—" She turned toward me. "The walls are the difficulty, then?"

"Yes. Defended as they are, they can withstand ten sieges."

"What if—what if Roman soldiers could get through those walls?"

"How? With black magic? They've tried scores of times. I pulled one of the firing ropes that helped turn them back."

She shook her head. "That's not what I meant. I know direct assault has failed. Still, there is one place—look!"

She pointed past the harbor to the place where the sea wall turned sharply inland.

"See that narrow tower on the spit of land where the walls bend? I know something about it because one of Archimede's slaves was assigned there as a guard. He told me of it one night when he returned to fetch some gear. It's a six-sided tower. That's why it's called the Hexapylum. Actually it's a watch tower for ships. Beacon lanterns are hung from the top in more peaceful times."

"What's the point, Cynthia? The tower is directly in range of the defense engines!"

"Of course it is," she agreed. "But it's also near a gate in the main wall. It's the most lightly patrolled of all the perimeter towers, and it has a sort of inner courtyard that's fairly well protected on either side by its own walls. From there, scaling ladders could be put up with relative safety. A few men could get over and open the wall gate. The rest could go straight through from the Hexapylum—"

"With the willing consent of the defenders, I suppose?"

She ignored the cynicism. "There is a time soon when the Hexapylum may be entirely undefended— and the wall gate behind it as well. I remembered that when I saw the tower a moment ago."

"What are you talking about?"

"Of all the gods and goddesses in our pantheon none is more sacred than the Virgin Huntress, Artemis. At the time of the full moon—not many days away now—there'll be a religious celebration. A nocturnal celebration, lasting from sunset to dawn. Nothing short of complete destruction of the city will keep the people of Syracuse from enjoying that night. If the Romans were to withdraw, seemingly beaten, and wait until the festival, and then attack—"

"Try to penetrate the Hexapylum then, you mean?"

"Yes."

I was ready to laugh at her pretensions at planning strategy. I did not do so because it was not such a far-fetched idea—*if* all that she told me was correct. Sometimes in the mounting of massive assaults, commanders overlooked the very simplest factors. It didn't entirely surprise me that a woman would be aware of them.

"Cynthia, do you suppose there'd be a heavy guard in that tower on the night of the festival?"

"Perhaps not, if it seems that the siege has been withdrawn."

"To try it—" Slowly, I pointed at the opposite shore. "Marcellus would have to know. Who would tell him?"

Of course I already knew the answer. It frightened me because I was so exhausted. The alternative, however, was to remain in this house, helpless and ineffectual, when there were Greeks I badly wanted to repay—

I gathered part of the chain in my hand, staring over the balustrade at the black water. I took a slow, deep breath, then asked:

"How deep is the sea down there?"

"Many times a man's height, but I don't see why—no, *Julius!* You could never swim across that bay. Especially not with the chain dragging on you!"

"Probably not. Very likely my head would pop open like a melon if I dove from this height. But if there were even one chance in ten thousand, I'd try. It would be better to be buried down there than wait for them to find me here and perhaps be forced to watch them punish you again."

"Forget what I suggested!" she pleaded. "The idea was worthless—" Then she looked closely at my face, and grew sad. "I have said it too late, haven't I, my darling? The seed's planted."

"Yes, but it happened long before this. It happened when they whipped and hurt you—"

To attempt it was folly, I knew; a madman's last, desperate gamble. Yet in war, many mad occurrences transpire. The Romans inside the walls—in possession of the siege engines of Archimedes for even an hour—might turn the tide.

And a military victory was my only chance to possess this lovely woman for more than a little while.

Quickly I kissed her, feeling her warmth against the burned flesh on my chest. She saw the set of my face, and her hands began to caress me with a sweet, sad hunger. My own hands soon responded.

Danger gives its own spice to lovemaking, brief and clumsy as it may be. And with the chain, it was clumsy indeed. Comical to any outside observer, I suppose. Yet never before had our union been so passionate—

Perhaps because we both understood full well that this time might be the very last.

Cynthia gave my hand a last fervent squeeze before I scrambled up on the terrace rail. I grew momentarily dizzy, contemplating the distance to the water. Were these the final seconds of my life—?

Despite that, I knew I must go.

"At the shrine in this house," she said, "I'll pray to my gods to help you, my darling. Pray they will—"

Suddenly she whirled toward a flare of light. Like ravening wolves, men were spilling through the house—

A soldier with a lantern appeared, speaking before he quite saw me against the starlight:

"My lady, we have entered through your garden. Quite a few Roman prisoners escaped from the wall. Several engines were damaged tonight, and in the confusion, the prisoners got away. We saw smears of blood on the door of your house, and on the garden wall as—*who is that with you?*"

He thrust around the light-bearer. "Zeus preserve us! Swords out, men! We've got one—"

He raced forward. I swung the heavy links in my right hand, ready to jump down to the terrace and defend her as the soldiers closed in.

But the mind of the woman I loved was as strong as mine. She cried.

"Tell your general, my darling!"

She pushed me over the edge of the rail.

Down and down, I went plummeting through the dark. She had wanted to save me, even if she herself might be lost—

The chain lashed my face. As I twisted and tried to right myself, I heard her scream out, piercingly. The scream was cut off an instant before I struck the black surface of the sea.

# CHAPTER IV

## TURNS OF FATE

A sharp prodding, repeated again and again, accompanied my slow return to consciousness. Unfamiliar faces
peered down at me—

"The tide washed this flotsam up, Centurion. I was
making my patrol as usual when I came across him on
the shore."

The faces came into focus. Roman faces; paler than
a Greek's. Helmets shone in the tattered, wind-blown
light of a torch.

"The commander—the general—" I began sense-
lessly. When I tried to stand, my legs buckled.

"Some Greek slave, obviously," the centurion said.
"Notice the ankle chain and disk—"

"Wonder what he expects from us? A purse of gold?
The few Greeks who have come over have proved
more treacherous than their masters—"

"The wind's too chilly to stand here chattering!" the centurion barked. "Get up, Greek. We'll put you in the prisoner compound like the rest of your thieving brethren. Too many weapons have disappeared for us to welcome you with open arms."

They manhandled me to my feet. I shook my head, fighting to stop the involuntary retching that began the moment I was upright. There was not a section of my body that was not bruised and hurting.

"Fetch Marcellus," I managed to gasp. "Fetch the commander. My name is Linus Julius. I am a legionary—"

The centurion and the beach guards frowned at one another. The former said, "What is this, some new Greek trick?"

"Fetch the general, damn you! I was captured in the first harbor assault and I—escaped from the siege machines inside the walls only tonight."

"He's not as dark as a Greek," one guard offered. "And he speaks the Latin, right enough."

The centurion snorted. "Do you suppose they'd send spies who didn't?"

"I am no spy!" I shouted, almost fainting from the exertion. "Find the general! He knows my face."

"Well, *I* don't," was the centurion's answer. "I'm grateful, too. I've never seen anyone uglier or dirtier—"

He gnawed his underlip. "Still, I don't precisely care to take the responsibility if by some remote chance you are telling the truth." He waved toward the torch-lit camp higher on the beach. "Nario, go fetch the first staff officer you can locate. We'll wait."

"Bring Marcellus!" I exclaimed. "I have important words for him."

"You'll talk to whomever we find!" the centurion snapped. "The general is making rounds in camp. But we'll get a senior officer to take charge of this matter."

And so the soldier did, with the assistance of the black fates which had lifted me up and helped me swim across that hellish harbor, only to smash me down again—

The soldier returned on foot. The silhouette of a mounted officer loomed behind him. Even before the officer rode into the light, I saw the stiffened, crippled left leg outthrust in the long stirrup.

*"No!"* I yelled. "This man won't listen to me. Get Marcellus and no one else!"

"That's *enough!*" the centurion bawled, slamming a fist against my temple. Everything whirled and spun. I landed on the damp sand, Pulvius and the centurion towering above me.

The latter explained the circumstances behind my then finished tale. "That's why I sent Nario to find a senior officer. I don't want to be the one to put him in the prisoner compound if he's truly a Roman."

"You acted correctly," Pulvius said, his voice smooth and his scarred face unreadable. "However, I fear you've been tricked. He is a Greek slave, and that's all he is."

"Liar!" The word came out feebly. "Centurion, this man will never admit the truth about—"

"Unpleasant-looking bit of sea scum too," Pulvius said loudly. "But a Greek."

*"He recognizes me! He knows who I am but he won't tell you because—"*

Pulvius interrupted:

"Take this raving fellow to the compound. Lock him up with the other deserters." He limped back to his

239

pawing mount and laboriously hoisted himself into the saddle. "Your attention in this matter won't go unnoticed, Centurion. This fellow is either an escaped slave or a spy." About to wheel away, he jerked his mount's head around and leaned toward me. "On second thought, we have no real use for Greeks in chains. They're merely burdens. And if he *is* a spy, we'll be better off without him. I suggest you use your sword here and now. Throw his body back into the water and be shed of him. Why should we waste another ration of food?"

At this, the centurion hesitated. "Sir, the regulations concerning captured Greeks stipulate—"

"Devil take the regulations: I've given you an order. Obey it!"

Flushing, the centurion hauled out his sword. Pulvius's mount danced in the fringe of the torchlight, as though catching some of his master's excitement over the sudden chance to have done with me for good.

The centurion hesitated, then signaled two of the beach guards. They laid hold of my shoulders. Pulled me to my feet—

"Push his head down," the centurion muttered. "Bare the back of his neck."

Up flashed the sword. I thought of Cynthia's face while the blade glittered—

The sudden sound of hoofbeats made Pulvius twist in his saddle. A tribune clattered up, his horse lathered.

"There you are, Pulvius!" he said. "The general's been searching for you everywhere. He wants to confer on a most urgent matter, and I am to bring—what in the world's going on here? Who is that man?"

240

"We caught a Greek spy," Pulvius said hastily. "I am ready to ride with you—"

The centurion's hand hesitated, the sword at the top of the arc. I yelled: "Tribune—Listen! I am a Roman like yourself. Bring Marcellus. He'll know!"

*"I tell you he's a Greek!"* Pulvius cried—too hysterically. The tribune's brow furrowed. He flung Pulvius's hand off his bridle:

"Be that as it may sir, something strange is happening, and your voice is a mite too shrill."

And he reared back on his horse, turned and pounded away along the beach, his cloak streaming behind him.

Pulvius trembled. Within moments, there came a clatter of many horses. Shortly Marcellus appeared, bareheaded and in full dress armor. He dismounted and strode forward, his craggy face cast into lines of annoyance.

"Now what is all this commotion about escaped Greeks? I have more on my mind than—" He stopped, peering at me. "Give me that torch."

He literally snatched it from the hand of the startled beach guard. He thrust it so near my face, my hair nearly caught fire.

"This man is no Greek! Under all that beard he's as much a Roman as you or I. Why is your sword drawn, Centurion?"

"I—I was merely—following orders—

*"Whose orders?"*

"Those of Sardus Pulvius. He assured me the fellow was a spy and instructed me to kill him."

Something peculiar and wary glinted out of Marcellus' iron eyes. He turned slowly. "Pulvius, dismount.

These men may not fathom what's been happening here. But I think I do. And it reeks."

For a moment I thought Pulvius would bolt. But he obeyed the stern voice of the commander, though he remained standing quite near his horse, his hand on the bridle.

The miserable centurion began again:

"General, I—I regret any mistake. But your officer told me he didn't know this person."

"Even though I tried to explain—and in Latin—who I was," I said.

Marcellus studied me over his shoulder. "Perhaps I know the reason for your difficulty, Prefect. Pulvius, did you really fail to recognize him? I thought he was well known to you."

Pulvius made a weak, uncertain gesture. "The unsteady light of the torches made it extremely difficult to—"

"*Nonsense!* I demand a better explanation."

Trembling with suppressed anger, he stalked up to Pulvius. "Or perhaps I can provide it myself. On the day the claws wrecked our galleys in the harbor, I saw you at the rail of my flagship. You and many others were tossing lines to men who wanted to save themselves. I saw you cast a line to this prefect I knew to be your enemy. A short cast. A *deliberately* short cast—one he never could have caught. In other words, I saw you consign him to the Greeks."

Finally the masks were down. Pulvius said rather weakly, "No, General, I meant to help him. But it was impossible."

"*You meant to let him drown or be taken prisoner!* I should have summoned you then and there. Made you pay the penalty. Fool that I was, I didn't. I assumed

242

the poor wretch was already dead. And to expose you would have spread ruinous disunity—"

Marcellus had walked very close to his officer. His voice grew steadily more wrathful:

"Since that day of shame and defeat, Pulvius— shame compounded by a filthy act of betrayal to a brother soldier—I've watched you carefully. I have waited for your first misstep, and at last I've been rewarded. I beg the forgiveness of the gods for being hoodwinked for so long by your glib tongue and fawning ways. *I'll show you how Rome repays an officer who allows a personal quarrel to interfere with his duty—*"

Almost beyond speech, he smashed the helmet from Pulvius' head. Then he tore the cloak from his shoulders and flung it to the sand.

"Sardus Pulvius, you are stripped of your rank and relieved of your duties. Guards, take this man to his quarters. Allow him only the run of the camp until I decide what other punishment he deserves."

The general's voice dropped to a new, threatening note:

"To betray the honor of the eagles is beyond all pardon. *Get out of my sight before I do damage to you myself!*"

Shrieking hysterical protests, Pulvius was pushed into the darkness. Marcellus turned back to me. His face, however, was not entirely friendly.

"As for you, Prefect—catch him, someone, *catch him!*"

The strain and the physical punishment had told at last. I sprawled on the sand once more, but this time I was swallowed by the healing dark.

# CHAPTER V

# TOWER OF TREACHERY

The ministrations of the camp surgeons—and perhaps the knowledge that the dice of the gods had been cast in my favor for a change—restored me to a semblance of myself within a day's time.

Smiths sawed away the shackles on my arm and ankle. That very same evening, the general agreed to receive me. Though I felt odd with clean skin, bandages and shaven cheeks, and my armor weighed strangely heavy after the weeks of captivity, I was nevertheless able to negotiate my way to Marcellus's pavilion unaided. I even downed a draft of his wine without growing lightheaded.

The general dismissed my words of thanks with a single wave. He asked for a detailed account of my misadventures since the ill-fated harbor attack. I told the story as briefly as I could, and included Cynthia's suggestion for infiltrating the tower.

"Which tower?" he asked, rather crossly. "There are a dozen ranged about the walls."

"The Hexapylum, General. The six-sided one on the point of land where the cliffs begin."

"Another of your woman's notions? She certainly has quite a hand in our affairs!"

"Only because she has been a part of mine."

"How can we be sure that what she says is trustworthy? Not just another Greek strategem?"

"Sir, she was whipped by her own half-brother. Then he ordered her turned out of her own house and dispossessed of everything. He reduced her to beggary. I doubt that she's anxious to help him so much as one iota."

Marcellus scratched his chin. "Perhaps, perhaps. Well, I'm ready to entertain almost any wild scheme that will make this siege go forward." He pondered a moment. "This Spartan you overheard on the platform—tell me more about him."

"Damippus was his name. Apparently he was going home to recruit volunteer troops to come to the aid of the Greeks. He planned to sail on tomorrow evening's tide—that is, tonight's."

Marcellus walked slowly to the pavilion entrance. He lifted the hanging, his thoughtful face silvered by the moon.

"Prefect, I'll be honest with you. The siege has gone abysmally. I have reached a point of desperation—" He threw me a keen glance whose meaning I couldn't fathom. "If I tried it, the timing would be very close. The tide turns a little more than an hour—" He spun

246

back to the entrance. "Orderly! Summon the staff! At once!"

I jumped up, frowning. "General, I don't follow your plan."

His craggy features changed then. A familiar, foxy smile appeared:

"Why, it's simple enough. Before we can attempt to penetrate Syracuse through the Hexapylum, we must learn all we can about the tower. But we can't accomplish that with ordinary skirmishing. Therefore the wolves must come robed as lambs. Perhaps we can suggest the vicinity of that tower as the ideal spot to hold another truce parley. Surely you recall how much I favor parleys as a means of delay—"

"Over what could we possibly parley, sir? Not surrender. That would be unthinkable."

"Is it?" Marcellus laughed. "Not at all—if we're talking about the surrender of a prisoner. An important prisoner—shall we say one like that Spartan, Damippus? If we're lucky, and my captains aren't all drunk, we can snare him at the harbor mouth when the tide turns!"

Soon the pavilion overflowed with staff officers. Before half an hour had passed, four galleys had put out from the coast and moored beyond the sight of the city's seawall.

Tense hours crawled by. When the galleys sailed past the camp shortly after dawn, they were towing a Greek trireme. She looked low and fast, built for speed rather than fighting. Signal pennants from the mast of the foremost Roman galley carried the message everyone awaited:

Damippus was captured.

That very day, Marcellus sent negotiators to the

headquarters of Hippocrates under a truce flag. The negotiators suggested that a parley dealing with prisoner exchange be held on the spit of land near the great six-sided tower. No objections were forthcoming. Wearing his finest ceremonial armor, Marcellus went to the meeting in person.

Though I was not privileged to go along, I later heard his performance had been masterful. He was an expert in the art of delay—Fabian tactics, as it was called in dubious honor of our hesitant dictator. Marcellus had quibbled and pondered over every phrase and inflection of the Greeks. His aim was to exchange all the Roman soldiers held captive in Syracuse for Damippus and his captured retinue.

The sessions dragged on. Every night Marcellus retired to a secret pavilion in the foothills, having first made certain there was a great show of lights and activity around his official tent, which the Greek defenders could easily see.

In the secret headquarters, Marcellus personally drew maps of the tower area as he had surveyed it earlier that day. I was at his side during these sessions, privileged to hear how fluently he talked with the engineers, who were readying yet another secret camp further back in the hills. There they were to prepare special collapsible scaling ladders.

The timing of the negotiations was a delicate affair. The moon waxed fuller every night. Soon it would be wholly round. On that night, the feast of Artemis would take place—and bring our last, best chance.

To tell the truth, I did not expect any results from the parley. I doubted the Greeks would surrender their entire force of captive labor. Yet such must have been the high station of Damippus in Sparta that they did just that. Marcellus artfully contrived to conclude the negotiations at sunset, the night before the full moon and the feast.

That evening the Roman camp rang with ribald laughter. Certain cohorts assigned to put on a show of revelry for the Greeks watching from the walls; a show indicating no siege could possibly be in the offing. Meantime another cohort of picked men was slipped into place behind the screen of sandy hills which hid the Hexapylum from the coastline on our side.

Marcellus had acceded to my request and permitted me to join the attack cohort. The day passed slowly. When the sun sank on the feast night and the moon rose white and fat, we were ready.

The general came riding up the beach shortly after sundown. He remained with us through the gathering of full darkness. Under cover of more boisterous noise from the Roman camp, the rest of the legion was poised to move at the proper signal. We were crouched behind the dunes, a short hour away from the start of the attack, when a mounted messenger came pounding up.

"General, a party of Greeks brought this scroll just now, under truce colors."

Flints were struck for fire. Marcellus knelt on the ground, reading by the light of a single small torch. Finally he rose and pushed past his officers:

"Prefect? *Prefect Julius!*"

His voice, no larger than a whisper, was enraged.

When I presented myself, he thrust the scroll into my hand.

"Gods! To think I put faith in some woman's clacking tongue!" he said furiously. "I deserve this bad luck for my insane stupidity."

I turned the scroll in the moonlight and with difficulty made out the characters. My veins froze as I ran down the lines one at a time:

*Lord Kyron herewith presents his respects and bids General Marcellus know that the woman to whom the escaped Roman L. Julius talked has been discovered. She has broken down under torture. She has revealed the plan of attack on the tower during feast night. Lord Kyron and his men await the general with anticipation. They bid the general tell the Roman L. Julius that the traitorous woman will perish tonight for her acts, taking her place among the numerous ritual sacrifices customarily offered to divine Artemis.*

The parchment fell from my hands. "General! She would never tell them anything!"

"Oh, you're sure, are you? Let's see how sure—"

He pulled his own broadsword and thrust it into my hand, his face full of contempt for me and for himself.

"You go first, Prefect. You go over that dune alone, into the Hexapylum. If we hear your screams ring out, we'll know who's right. Will we not?"

Still shaking, he stood aside and pointed over the moonlit hill.

His sword in my hand, I had no choice but to turn through the ranks of sullen men and go as he bade, to scout alone.

# CHAPTER VI

## *"FOR THE REPUBLIC!"*

Across the massive walls of the Greek city so peaceful and white in the full moon, faint voices drifted, raised in some haunting but alien religious chant. Then came the mournful blowing of the ceremonial horns. The hilt of the general's fine blade turned slick with sweat in my hand.

I dropped my cloak near the top of the dune. It would only encumber me. Again the strange, lonesome horn blew within the city. Kyron's parchment had talked of death for Cynthia. My belly was hurting at the thought.

I glanced back down the dune. Stretched away in the darkness, the huddled shadows of the legionnaries waited. Moonlight blazed on Marcellus' armor and silvered his grizzled head. His face was in darkness. I was glad I could not see it. The only way to prove Cynthia hadn't betrayed him through me—and the only way to learn whether Kyron's grim promise of her sacrifice was true as well—was to reach the Hexapylum and learn the truth myself.

So I dropped on my belly, crawling on knees and elbows through the damp sand. The hexagonal tower rose against the moon. From the last dune before the open space separating me from it, I peered into the shadows at its base. I saw nothing; heard nothing—

Far to the left and right on the rampart of the city wall, I saw a sentry. The screams of revelers deep within Syracuse sounded more loudly every moment. My heart hurt from beating so fast. Cynthia's tormented face haunted me again—

I tried to think of the tower. From the courtyard on the far side, our men could raise the special ladders which were the exact height to reach the battlements. There was need to assault a wall gate—

Cautiously, I crawled across the open area to the tower, and listened at its outer door for a considerable time. If there had been men inside, I would have heard a few faint sounds. There were none. Kyron's forces, if they were hidden there, must be ghosts.

For many minutes I remained by the tower, struggling to find the answer to the riddle of a Greek army which was capable of absolute silence. Suddenly I recalled something about Kyron's scroll—

"She told the truth!" I said, half aloud. "She told the truth and yet she didn't. That must be it!"

With my hopes rising once more, I raced back over the dunes and rejoined Marcellus who was waiting impatiently.

"General, the Hexapylum is empty."

"Did you go inside?"

"No, but I'm positive—"

"Prefect," he interrupted, "I will not send these men to be slaughtered on your say-so. Not this time."

"General, I swear I'm right! I think I know now where Kyron's men have gone—or at least why they're not here. May I see the scroll?"

Reluctantly, he passed it over. I studied it a moment.

"General, look. Kyron's own words— *She has revealed the plan of attack on the tower during feast night.* There is no mention of the Hexapylum. None! Remember when I first suggested the plan, you asked me which tower I meant? You noted there are a dozen round about the walls. I think Kyron's message is true. I think they tortured her, and that she probably told them about the attack. *But I don't think she told them the right tower!*"

Marcellus's dim face showed a hope he didn't quite dare to accept. "There's one way to learn for certain." He spun and issued orders to a subordinate. Within moments, the spectral figures of half a dozen scouts glided away into the night.

Three of them returned in a short time, having found nothing. The fourth brought the news that I'd prayed for:

"At the Octagonal gate tower, Commander. Six down the line from this one. I distinctly heard armor rattling, and some officer hushing his men. In Greek. How many are waiting there, I can't say. But I'm certain it's more than a few."

Slowly, Marcellus rolled up Kyron's document. Then his craggy head lifted, his eyes sought mine and he said softly:

"Not often does a general beg the pardon of a soldier of lesser rank. But I beg yours now. Whatever happens to the lady, she'll be remembered for the way she helped us."

Then, like a great bear who has scented the blood of weaker prey, he flung Kyron's parchment into the sand.

"First maniple with ladders—*forward!* But not a sound until we top the wall."

A file of black shapes slipped across the sand and into the Hexapylum. I followed Marcellus through the tower into the oblong courtyard where whispers and a faint scrape of wood broke the quiet of the night as the engineers hastily lashed their ladders together and braced them against the inner wall. The lonely sentries on duty to the right and left along the wall heard nothing. Somewhere in the city, the ceremonial horns blew again.

Marcellus clapped a soldier on the back and sent him up the ladder. Then another, then scores—all climbing fast and silently.

Abruptly, the shadows of hunched men broke the clean line of the battlements. The sentry far to the left was first to spot the attackers dashing toward him. He died with a sword through his belly, his scream never leaving his throat. Someone pushed his body off the wall.

Marcellus breathed with great loud gulping sounds. This was the aim of all his training—to win for the Republic. And at last the fates had smiled upon him.

Inside the great wall, metal squealed faintly. A bar rattled. The gate opposite the courtyard of the Hexapylum creaked back—

The way was open.

Behind me, the Hexapylum was crowded with a

hundred men. They poured through, followed by a hundred more, then another hundred, until the courtyard seemed like some channel through which a great black tide was rushing to the sea.

For several minutes Marcellus watched the host streaming by. Then he took his helmet from the crook of his arm and set it on his head. To an orderly standing near he said:

"Now, soldier, speed to the camp. Bring every last man, even those who've remained behind to sing and keep the fires lit. Through this one needle's eye, we'll run a rope to strangle Hannibal."

The orderly raced away. Sudden shouts and the clang of steel beyond the wall told me our men had met their first opposition. Marcellus laughed low and said:

"Well done, Prefect. They can never stand against us in terms of numbers, only with their huge walls and machines. Now the walls are breached. Find yourself some Greeks to kill, because by sunrise there'll be none left. Now I'll thank you for my sword."

Lifting it from my hand, he joined the stream of men rushing into the avenue. I saw him turn in the moonlight, raise the blade and cry, *"For the Republic!"*

There was silence no longer. Wild yells ripped from every Roman's throat. The iron tide engulfed everything before it.

I pushed my way through the narrow gate and joined a band of running men. With one victory in sight, there must be a chance to gain a second, and to find Cynthia before they killed her.

Marcus Claudius Marcellus was a general who knew when the tide was running with him. As he had predicted, breaching the walls was the deciding factor in the outcome of the siege.

Within an hour of the penetration of the Hexapylum, sections of both outer quarters of Syracuse were afire, put to the torch by legionnaries burning out isolated pockets of resistance. Like animals caught in a wind-fanned blaze, most ordinary citizens who had remained in the outer sections during feast night had fled. The corpses of the unfortunate few who had not lay piled at street corners.

Every Roman soldier in the entire Sicilian host was turned loose within two hours' time. The major portions of Syracuse fell with only minor casualties on our side. Only the central city remained as a final challenge.

Greeks massed on its walls with bows, spears, and even weapons such as kitchen pots. After a brief engagement at one point on the perimeter of this wall, Marcellus ordered the legions to fall back several blocks.

I fought my way through close-packed men who waited for orders in the narrow streets. Far ahead, the central wall stood out plainly, illuminated by the torches of the Greek defenders.

"What's the reason for this delay?" I asked. "Why aren't we moving forward?"

"General's orders," an officer replied. "We're to hold our places and keep silence."

"Orders?" I retorted. "The Greeks are trapped inside that one quarter, and they're outnumbered. We have only to put up the ladders, go over the wall, and take them. We've got five times the men!"

"It's not my doing," replied the officer gruffly. "The word was passed down from the Main Standard. Marcellus won't storm the central quarter for two hours yet—perhaps three. Don't ask me to explain any further. They didn't explain it to me either."

In the heat of the crowded thoroughfare with sparks from burning buildings falling all around, I knew that Marcellus had some plan in mind. What it was, I couldn't say. Nor did I care. Cynthia was uppermost in my thoughts now. There was only one path for me to follow—

I must somehow enter that central quarter myself.
Immediately.

# CHAPTER VII

# *DEATH-SMILE*

To do it would require more than my sword and a scaling ladder, I soon realized. Going over the wall would be impossible for a single Roman soldier.

Yet there *had* to be a way—

It was then I thought of the house of Archimedes by the sea wall. If the gods gave me luck, the old man might be there tonight instead of revelling with the others. It was no better than an even chance, but I had no other. I might find him sleeping, or musing on his arcane philosophies. Or I might not find him at all. But I must look—

I struggled against the sea of marchers calling, "Let me through! Let me pass! I carry dispatches for the commander!" Then the gods turned on me again.

A horse neighed and its rider jerked the reins. "Prefect Julius! *Over here!*"

I swung around. Riding in with a fresh company—

let loose because this was a triumphant night or merely unwatched and roaming abroad, I knew not which—I saw Pulvius.

His scarred face was a grotesque landscape of light and shadow in the glare of the pitch-pine torches being carried by. He turned out of the column, climbed from his saddle and limped toward me. I put my hand on my sword hilt and waited, standing close by a wall. This encounter had been a long time coming. Perhaps the fates intended it as a final test for both of us.

I could vividly recollect what the man approaching me had done. The humiliations, the attempts at murder, all passed before my mind in a kind of swift and hazy panorama. In my time I had killed and I had spared life; I had won some praise and a good deal of abuse. In those moments I would have traded all of it for a certainty that I win out against Sardus Pulvius now, and have his head.

"*Ave*, Prefect!" he said, pausing a few feet away, his left leg awkwardly positioned. "Tonight they freed the dogs from their cages to let them watch the show. I almost remained behind in camp. There's nothing left for me in this army now—except remembering who penned me up in the first place."

Soldiers rushed by, mounted and on foot. None looked at us as they hurried ahead to their standards. Pulvius began walking toward me again. I closed my eyes, sick over Cynthia and the delay, yet knowing he would follow if I ran. I turned and began moving down a cross street, pitch dark like the underworld itself. After a few paces, I turned around again.

Pulvius' great shadow loomed on the cobbles. The blade in his hand glared bright. Clumsily, he moved his crippled left leg forward one step, then another.

"There are kind winds of fortune still blowing after all." His voice bounced eerily off the walls. "Tonight they pushed us down that avenue there, instead of another. They gave me what I never thought I'd have again—the chance to face you, the dung-man who robbed me. *Robbed me of everything—*"

Then he lunged.

The passing torches reflected some spittle on his lips. He was a madman at that moment, a madman without rank, honor or even sense. He was stripped of all humanity, and all that was left to him was his sword and his desire to kill.

I backed against the wall. Flung up my blade to parry. Iron met iron with a great ring and a sputter of blue sparks. He grunted softly as I hurled him away. Then he laughed and began to close again, his scarred face floating like a death-mask in that grim place.

I retreated a step. Another. Suddenly my back bumped the wall—

Pulvius drew his right arm to his left shoulder, then brought it chopping forward to slice off my head. I ducked, aiming my own sword at his gut. His blade whistled over my head.

My boots skidded in street slime. Pulvius changed direction in mid-stroke, cutting downward. He missed. Iron struck the cobbles, a loud clatter. Panting, he fell back, his lips still wrenched into a deranged smile.

"Very quick—" he panted. "You are very quick but then—so is the rat when—the cat—*jumps*—" He hurled his whole body at me.

I leaped to one side. His blade sped by my belly with just a whisper to spare. I saw a chance to strike his side. I drove in with all the force I possessed—

He seemed to shudder to a halt, shivering. Then he realized there was iron in him; killing iron. He threw his head back and gave one damned, demented cry:

"No, not to a man lowborn—no!"

The cry keened up into a long, bestial wail. Even dying on his feet with his scarred cheeks worm-white and twitching, he managed to bring his sword around and cut at my arm one last time. This time his blow did not miss.

I tore my blade out of his belly and reeled back, blinded by the pain. Blood washed down my whole left side. Slowly he crumpled into the trickle of running water in the street. Soldiers still rushed by on the avenue and never saw.

The dark eyes of Sardus Pulvius flew open and met mine. His mouth wrenched again, a ghastly parody of a smile. His stiff leg kicked once and the death-rattle came out of his grinning mouth and he was still.

My belly seemed to threaten to rise up my windpipe. Pain tormented me. The stroke to my arm had been deep. With my teeth and right hand, I used part of his cloak to bind the wound. Then I turned back to the avenue and crossed between the marchers pouring down to their standards near the inner wall.

My step faltered. Sardus Pulvius was dead but my victory began to seem empty. Even in death he rode with me, and perhaps he'd won the final race of all. Stumbling along in the dark, I wasn't sure but what his stroke would finish me long before I reached my goal. Moment by moment, the blood was draining out beneath the improvised bandage, weakening me—

Perhaps the gods had whispered that to Pulvius as he died. Perhaps that was why he could still laugh.

# CHAPTER VIII

# IN THE TEMPLE OF ARTEMIS

The trail of gore that I left while climbing Archimedes' garden wall was blacker and wider than the last time. I tumbled on the grass on the other side, for a moment too utterly spent to rise. Then the memory of her— what might happen to her this night—drove me to my feet.

The houses on the city's outer perimeter had been left relatively unscathed. That was the case with the great *domus* of Archimedes. I hurried through room after silent room, hurling furniture out of my way as I shouted, "Old man! Answer if you're here! I won't hurt you—"

In a chamber off the atrium, I thought I saw a flicker of yellow. Unsteadily, I went that way. Suddenly hangings parted. His spindly shape loomed up, his white beard fluttering as he shook with surprise and

263

alarm. He saw blood on the military trappings and took me for an attacker. A small knife in his left hand gleamed.

"Leave this house, soldier. I have no quarrel with you, but I'll kill you if I must."

"Archimedes, look at my face!" I thrust around him into the light from the inner chamber. "I am the soldier Julius. Cynthia's soldier. She's on her way to her death tonight, if it hasn't happened already. In the name of heaven put up the knife and *listen*. I must get into the central quarter and I can't do it alone."

He blinked in a rather baffled way, his old eyes watering. "How can you think about her when your own comrades are bathing in blood?"

"I have no more taste for this slaughter than you. It's only Cynthia that I care about. That fine, noble officer, Kyron, is going to have her killed." Leaning on the doorframe, dizzy, I managed to give the message of his scroll. "Marcellus won't attack the central wall for some time yet. So if her friendship meant anything at all to you, tell me how to get in there."

At last fits of trembling passed, and he gave attention to the problem: "Well, let me see— From time to time there are sacrifices to the Virgin Huntress in a private temple in the king's palace. That might be the location. For you to reach it alone would be impossible. However, if it were not you who sought refuge there, but an old man fleeing the enemy—an old man caught by surprise in his house on the sea wall when the battle commenced—"

Suddenly he began to quiver again; with excitement this time, I thought.

"Are you strong enough to help me hitch a horse, Roman? There's one in the stable, I believe. If we can ready the chariot and find the gate to pass into the central quarter, then I know the back ways and passages leading to the temple."

"I'll follow you," I said. "I'll follow you until I fall dead behind you. Just help me find her."

"I will. She is my friend too."

In a ramshackle building at the edge of the villa grounds, we found a spindly horse in a stall and man-handled him into the traces. Then I climbed into the car and huddled down. Archimedes covered me with a rank-smelling robe and ordered me to remain absolutely quiet.

The chariot lurched off. Each turn of the wheel jarred me with fresh pain. The trip seemed endless. Several times the chariot rocked, and once it threatened to overturn. At last, with a scream of metal wheels on stone, it swayed to a halt.

"Leap down!" He tore the robe aside. "Those stairs yonder lead to the temple passage."

The sword in my fist weighed like a stone. I stumbled after him, up a dark flight which brought us to a door with an iron ring. Before we plunged into the sprawling palace building, I had a glimpse of Greek fighting men gathering outside its low ornamented wall, building barricades against the coming Roman on-slaught. Beyond that, the outer quarter was a sea of burning rooftops.

"Push your shoulder against the door," Archimedes said. "I don't have the strength to move it by myself."

The door was unbarred but ponderous. My body broke out with fresh bursts of pain at the effort. But we moved it at last.

We entered a narrow, low-ceilinged passage lit with

oil lamps. Our running feet raised flat, eerie echoes. Abruptly the old man gripped my arm:

"This alcove here to the right. There's another ring in that floor block. Quickly, now—quickly!"

Together we tugged at the heavy metal circle and lifted the stone. Archimedes led the way down the short stair into a chill underground tunnel, explaining:

"This passage is used by city women who sometimes come to mingle with the priests. The rites—well, there's no point in talking about those just now. Suffice it to say that this entrance is not employed by persons of high moral character—"

As we rounded the last turn in the passage, loud voices reached us. Ahead I saw lights beyond thin hangings. Archimedes let out a cry of dismay as I dashed forward through the curtains. I paid no attention, for it no longer mattered whether two or two hundred waited for me. I was too deep into the city to escape, and sick with pain and fear; nearly beyond rational thought.

The loud voices broke off. A woman screamed. None in that chamber, I suspect, was prepared for the sight of a filthy, blood-smeared Roman soldier stumbling through an opening in the wall.

The high-ceilinged temple chamber had been hewn from bedrock. At one end stood a lamplit altar beneath a graven image of Artemis, the full-breasted virgin goddess who held a gilt bow in one hand. The altar had old stains on it; many stains, dark and dried.

Details struck my mind in that when I tottered there, the torn-down hangings half wrapped around my body. I saw a cowering group of men and women surrounded by several priests. Among this terrified band of sacrifices, the men with shaved heads, the women with bare breasts, one woman stood haughtily, trying not to show her fear—

For a moment, violet eyes burned with disbelief. Then Cynthia broke and began sobbing.

"Seize that man!" someone shouted. "I know him!"

Praying that I would stay alive for a moment, I wheeled around toward the source of the sound, and I saw him:

"Yes, you should know me well, Lord Hippocrates. We've been meant to meet like this for a long time."

*"Kyron!"* the general howled, backing off. "However he managed to get in here, *we must get rid of him!"*

"We will," the young noble snarled, taking out his sword. "We waited, Roman. We waited at the Octagonal tower where that bitch yonder said that you and your general would attack."

"But we came another way, lord. To find you and your butcher-king."

Hippocrates pushed past his lieutenant, whose very uncertainty showed that he saw murder in my eyes. Kyron didn't want to charge me singlehanded. Except for the sacrificer and the priests, one of whom wore a dark hooded mantle and lingered far back by the altar, there were no other men in the temple. Three of the priests carried spears, however.

Hippocrates pointed to Archimedes. "So you are responsible for his presence here."

"That is right."

"You filthy damned *traitor!"* Hippocrates spun toward the priests. "Why are you standing idle? He is only one soldier. Use your knives and spears. Get the work done!"

"No!" someone else said. "Do not kill him just yet. After a long time, I find that I know him too."

The name they had given him in Carthage meant Thunderbolt. It was fitting, for when he spoke, it was as if a thunderbolt had struck in the heart of that foul place.

He strode forward from the shadows around the altar and threw back the hood of the cloak. A gold hoop like a mariner's dangled from his left earlobe, winking in the light. He wore no other trappings of office. Only the face, the short clipped beard, the intense and never-to-be-forgotten-eyes said *Hannibal is here!*

"Lord," Hippocrates exclaimed to him, "this man is our enemy! How could you know a Roman soldier?"

"From Cannae," said Hannibal Barca. "From Cannae a long time ago."

He moved around in front of me, his bright eyes strangely speculative.

"What a long route we've both traveled, Roman, to end here with the city dying around us, and dreams and plans as well. How did you come to this place?"

Now Archimedes presented himself, his ancient face a study in fury as a result of the insults of Hippocrates. The priests waited like leashed dogs, gripping their spears and knife hilts. Time seemed to stop in that alien temple watched by the gilt eyes of the goddess.

"You are Hannibal Barca?" Archimedes whispered. "A man or a ghost?"

"A little of both," Hannibal said with some bitterness.

"My lord!" Hippocrates cried, trying to create a diversion. "This is the philosopher who built the engines. Now he has obviously betrayed us—"

"Be silent and let him speak!" Hannibal said.

"How is it that you're here?" Archimedes asked.

"I came secretly, on a fast galley waiting by the sea
268

wall. So you are the renowned Archimedes, eh? The errant genius to whom I owe what little hope I had for protecting Syracuse as a supply port. Well, whether your heart was in the defense or not, I thank you. I only wish that your labors had been better rewarded."

Archimedes met the Punic general's eye courageously.

"Lord, they say you are a fine soldier. More important, they say that you are an honorable man. Therefore I appeal to you to hold these power-crazed men at bay. Don't let them proceed with this useless sacrifice. No god or goddess can help us now. Syracuse is finised—and I can tell from your face that you know it. That woman—the one with the dark hair watching us—is sought by this Roman because he cares for her. She is to be killed only because Hippocrates hates her. And I repeat—no amount of sacrificial blood can save the city now."

While Hippocrates and Kyron exchanged looks of rage, Hannibal gave a slow nod:

"I know that. I think I began to realize it when Damippus failed to appear for our rendezvous at sea. When his ship never came, I decided I had to know the state of the siege. I decided to sail here myself. Secretly, the way the Roman may remember that I go among my own troops. My army is waiting in Latium for food and, more important, for hope. I can bring them neither now. Still, I must return to them—"

"Exactly!" Hippocrates cried. "Return to them and leave the affairs of Syracuse to me! The matter of this Roman's is mine alone to deal with. You must understand, my lord—that woman, the one the soldier seeks, betrayed us tonight. She told us Marcellus would attack by one gate but he came in at another."

Across his shoulder I glimpsed Cynthia's face. Her violet eyes told me that whatever might happen, she loved me, and that she had withstood their torturing for the sake of that love—

Sweaty-faced and anxious, Hippocrates continued to plead with the tall Carthaginian:

"Take yourself to the passage, lord! I am concerned about your safety if you remain—"

Hannibal's voice grew cold:

"Is it really my safety that concerns you? Or my displeasure—no, let's be clear—my anger over your bungling?"

Hippocrates swallowed hard. "Lord, I *can* save the city! If I can get you to go down to the harbor by the underground way and trust me! We'll kill this woman and the rest of these sacrifices, and then the gods will bring us good fortune."

The palm of Hannibal's great hand crashed into his cheek, rocking him. The Carthaginian's composure was shattered:

*"Is this how you do battle on my behalf? Is this how you defend my supply lines? No wonder you've lost the port if you wage war on women and depend on human sacrifice to bring you victory!"*

"Priests!" Hippocrates shrieked. "Put a knife into the first sacrifice! I'm still in command here, not this Punic—"

Before a single priest could stir, Archimedes walked across the chamber. He took a place beside the huddled crowd of victims and turned his face to us, a very old man who was ludicrously frail. Yet in that moment, there was a powerful strength, even a certain majesty about him.

The old man's voice was surprisingly forceful:

"Tell your priests to strike me first, Hippocrates. Only that way will you claim your victims. You have destroyed Syracuse for the sake of your ambition. You won't take any more lives for such a pathetic reason—

"*Priests!* I *order* you to—"

"Yes, order them!" the old man cried. "Order them to strike the sorcerer Archimedes! They will not."

And it was true. Hippocrates raged and ranted but the priests remained in their places, as if they feared that slaying the philosopher would release all the devils of the underworld.

What happened next took place so suddenly, no one could move to prevent it. Hippocrates leaped at Archimedes and drove his own dagger into the old man's chest.

Archimedes tumbled backwards. Blood poured down the front of his threadbare tunic. Women among the sacrifices began to wail again. I would have moved, but one man was faster—Hannibal of Carthage.

He flung back his cloak, his fury bursting forth in a thunderous oath. Like a blade of fire, a sword from beneath his cloak burned in the lamplight. Hippocrates threw up his hands. He could not stop the sword. It went through his bowels and out his back.

Kyron rushed to help his master. One swipe of Hannibal's blade lopped off his head. The ghastly ball rolled away across the floor. Silence fell.

The wrathful trembling drained out of Hannibal then. He closed his eyes for a moment, as if in extreme pain. He flung the sword on the stone floor.

"Fools and madmen," he whispered. "Fools and madmen have ruined me. They struck down the very genius who held the city for them."

And after one pitying look at the savant who lay in a pool of his own blood, he turned on me:

"I don't recall your name, Roman. But I recall you once swore to kill me because you thought I was a butcher. Now perhaps you understand what I think of butchery. Sometimes, to prevent it, I have been forced to practice it. Well—" A weary shrug. "Such is the way of the world. If I have brought you any measure of justice tonight—if I have kept those men and women from dying worthlessly on that altar—it was because of what that damned Greek general has done to me. And to my hope of victory. This night's work has done the cause of Carthage irreparable harm. With the loss of Syracuse, the war in Latium is all but finished. One day your Republic will drive me back to Africa. One day after that—who knows?"

There was a lonely magnificence about him as he shrugged again and slowly shook his head. I think he saw greatness slipping away in those brief seconds. He had let his honor speak more forcefully than his concern for the fate of Carthage. Softly, he added:

"One last favor, Roman. Don't judge me according to what people say about me. That I'm a monster. A butcher. Judge me by what you saw here tonight."

And with his shabby cloak belling around him, he turned and raced for the dark mouth of a passage behind the altar.

That was when the poor victims huddled near the priests finally realized their lives might be spared. They took heart and they took action. They fell on their captors. The priests died with throats and eyes torn out.

Moments later, the men and women were streaming for the barred temple doors. Lifting the great wooden cross pieces and hurling them aside, they fled to freedom. Only Cynthia remained behind.

The smell of blood was thick as I stumbled toward her. She stood gazing down at the body of Archimedes, not even able to weep any longer. In the instant I reached her, the thunder began—

There was a crash, then a terrible grinding and roaring. The temple walls shook. A lamp toppled off the altar. A drapery began to burn. The image of Artemis vibrated.

I stared up at a cloud of dust drifting from the ceiling, pulling Cynthia close. At last I knew why Marcellus had delayed his attack. He hadn't deemed it necessary to waste the lives of Roman soldiers to breach the wall of the inner quarter.

"The engines—" I whispered. *"He's turned the engines around."*

Somewhere a great stone struck the palace. A section of the temple wall near the ceiling sheared away. The statue of the goddess tipped forward slowly and smashed into a thousand gilt pieces. Frantic, I thrust Cynthia toward the door. The wall mortaring crumbled away as the engines hit and hit again, thunder upon thunder. Altar lights spilled oil everywhere. Hangings caught fire. In a moment we were running through billows of smoke and a hail of falling rock.

We were but halfway to the temple doors when the great lintel tumbled, bringing down all the blocks above it and closing that route of escape.

"The passage Archimedes used—!" I shouted, dragging Cynthia along. A rock struck my shoulder. We had almost reached the entrance in the wall when I heard a feeble cry. I spun, searching the smoke—

"The old man! *Cynthia, he is still alive—!*"

And so he was. I saw him struggling to rise amid the falling debris. I left her at the wall by the secret entrance and ran to help him. Just as I lifted the old, spindly body in my arms, Cynthia's shriek tore out.

When I faced her through the smoke, I saw why she had screamed. A huge, irregular chunk of masonry had crashed down in front of the secret entrance. Wildly, I faced around to the altar, but the passage which Hannibal had used was no longer even visible behind a mountain of fallen stone.

Every path of escape from the temple was sealed.

Placing Archimedes at Cynthia's feet, I threw myself against the jagged block of masonry barring the secret passage. When the block would not budge, I howled and beat my fists against it.

The chamber hangings were all afire now, hellishly bright. The smoke gagged us. Archimedes moaned and held to Cynthia's leg like a child while the monster engines he had created flung boulder after boulder from the outer walls.

With blood and tears on my face, I stared at Cynthia for an instant that seemed as long as all eternity. She leaned against me, trembling. All I could say was:

"I can't move it. We're trapped."

Another huge section of the ceiling crashed down. Bits of flying rock stung our faces. Fire and thunder all around us, I knew that we were done.

# CHAPTER IX

# TO MOVE THE EARTH

"Try again!" Cynthia pleaded in that nightmare of noise and light. "Try, Julius—!"

"It's solid. Not big, but heavy," I gasped. "No use. "No use—"

But the fright in her eyes struck me so profoundly, I did try, only to meet failure again. My eardrums hurt from the roar and the temple crumbling. When I shrugged to show the futility of trying to dislodge the block, she said something. I could not hear what it was.

Archimedes stirred. She knelt beside him. His eyes came open, glazed and childlike. He must have recognized Cynthia, because he seized her fingers and pressed them to his cheeks.

A stifling cloud of mortar dust fell around us, doubling me in a fit of coughing. When I straightened again, Cynthia had turned away and covered her face, her back bowed in some final agony. I soon saw why.

Archimedes lay rigid; dead.

I hated him in that moment. To help him, we had turned back when the escape route was still open. And thus he had consigned us to death along with himself.

The time which passed then could not have been long. Yet it seemed as if my thoughts floated free in some limbo where time was nothing at all. I recalled the first time I had set eyes on Cynthia, on the Lentini highroad when her chariot overturned.

I stumbled to her and buried my head on her shoulder. Her hands slipped around my neck. In the crumbling ruin around us, there was nothing else for either of us to do.

Across her shoulder I saw the lined cheeks of the poor dead stargazer. I thought of how I'd met him the first time, in his palace apartments, where he had been busy upsetting globes with a rod and block and—

After that, I do not recall leaving Cynthia's side, nor running across the temple. I do recall picking up a smaller stone which I found somewhere among the rubble. I wedged it up next to the larger block of masonry which blocked the passage.

I have a memory—fragmentary—of dragging an iron spear from beneath a pile of stones where a priest's head stuck from a scarlet jelly that was his crushed chest.

Cynthia looked at me as though I were mad. I forced the thick butt end of the spear beneath the large obstructing rock, then leaned my weight on the other end. The mid-point of the spear rested across the smaller stone.

I pushed and dragged on that spear, pushed and

dragged, calling to her in the tumult, "He said he could move the world with a place to rest the lever—"

But she could not hear. She was crying again. Gazing at nothing while she hugged her arms across her naked breasts.

The spear began to bend in the middle, at the place where it rested on the smaller rock.

Harder I pushed down, harder.

*Harder—*

Blood beat like a river about to break out through the dikes of my temples. My eyes felt like living things that stood out from my head. My wounded arm throbbed and poured out fresh blood—

Abruptly I jerked my head up. Overhead, another loud crackling and grinding signalled that the whole roof of the temple was beginning to go. Seconds of time were all that were left—

*But the larger stone seemed to be shifting—*

Then Cynthia backed against the wall. Terror shone in her eyes. Someone or something was behind me—

I twisted my head. Out of the rubble, twitching forward out of some primeval lust for revenge, came Hippocrates the Greek. His fine robes were torn and stained with blood and dust and mortar. There was a knife in his hand.

A gout of fire licked out, nearly burning his face. Still he came on, brandishing the knife. The ceiling rumbled again, ready to give. A large chunk tore loose and fell—

The agony of thrusting downward on the spear was unbearable. Yet I kept at it, pushing and pushing until the larger rock shifted again. It was triangular and if its balance could be altered in the right way, it might—

A sudden gust of fire seared my back. Smoke tormented my lungs. I had strength for only one last push.

From the grave, Archimedes reached out to us. The power of his mind was in the lever-spear that moved the stone just the narrowest margin. A draft of damp air washed over me. *There was an opening now*—small between the rock and the passage; but an opening. Cynthia stumbled toward it.

Hippocrates had fallen. He rose and came on again. Sparks caught in his hair. It began to burn. Still he kept walking. I squeezed into the narrow opening through which Cynthia had already slipped. But it was harder for me to get through. Skin ripped away from my arm as I twisted and wrenched, caught between the temple wall and an outcrop of the big rock thrusting against my belly.

Hippocrates reached me then. His mouth twisted into obscene curses that went unheard. The dagger raked my face as I jerked my body backward, trying to dislodge myself from that prison between stone and stone.

I ripped the flesh off my shoulder. He raised the knife to strike. I managed to get a grip on his arm. I broke his wrist, caught the falling knife and shoved the point into his right eye.

He shrieked, all his hair afire now. He fell backwards with the knife sticking from his eyesocket and disappeared under a new cascade of falling rock.

Cynthia's frantic hands around my neck tore me loose. I fell into the tunnel with her, conscious that my belly had been ripped half open by the jagged stone. Faintly I heard her crying out that we must run. I remember doing so, down that long black passage.

Still the noise increased, mounting into a cataclysm

of sound that I could not separate from the roaring in my own ears.

*We have not gone far enough,* I thought. *Cynthia, we are not far enough away—*

There was one final clap of engulfing thunder, then blackness.

# CHAPTER X

# SOLDIER'S FAREWELL

After enduring great pain, fear of pain is no longer possible. So it was when I opened my eyes in a rust-colored sunset and saw Greek surgeons bending beside my pallet.

As they began to speak, I noticed a Roman sentry behind them. Somewhere the evening's bugle note rose up sweet and clear. Long years in the legion had taught me the pattern of the notes. It was a Roman trumpet call.

We had run far enough in that tunnel after all. Later I learned we had been discovered by legionnaries swarming into the half-demolished palace to raise the golden standard of the Republic from the highest tower still standing in Syracuse.

Soon Cynthia came to sit beside me. Her eyes were still haunted by memories of what we had experienced.

But her body was whole and her lips were warm against my cheek.

As the days passed and I mended slowly, I heard what had happened after Syracuse surrendered.

The dark galley on which Hannibal Barca had made his secret inspection visit had escaped to sea. By now he had returned to his host in Latium. Jubilant couriers sped to the Senate in Rome, carrying the news that Hannibal's supply line had been severed at last. This circumstance, as it turned out, was the beginning of the end of his campaign in Roman territory—exactly as he had predicted in the temple. Although Hannibal lived many years, he never won another battle. Before my time on earth is over, I feel sure that Scipio the Younger, a fiery general they are already beginning to call Africanus, will march into Carthage and burn it out, removing its threat forever.

But as I rested on my pallet in the temporary hospital established in the palace ruins, I knew none of this. For the moment, other tales filled the drowsy hours between long sleeps:

Tales of Roman barbarism were spread to explain the death of Archimedes, and to conceal that he was in fact slain by one of his own people. There was also a happier story abroad, and it was a truthful one: the two banished legions had been granted full pardon by Marcellus; given back their eagles and their rightful places as part of the regular army of the Republic.

Then came the day when one of the surgeons paused at my bedside.

"Are you strong enough for some bad news, Prefect? That arm of yours—the one that somebody hacked for you—" I stared up at him in silence, thinking of Pulvius. "—several of the muscles are ruined. Indeed we had to fight to save the arm from amputation."

I said, "It has felt much weaker than the other. Wooden, almost."

"I'm afraid it will always be so. That's regrettable, since a fighting man needs a strong arm. Still, it's better to lose the use of an arm than to lose your life—"

I turned my face to the wall.

Shortly one of Marcellus's officers arrived. He bore a letter of commendation from the commander. Then he gave me another piece of news. I had been promoted to centurion in the Fourth Legion.

"With this?" I asked him bitterly, pointing to the ruined arm. "Surely the promotion is some cruel joke—"

He smiled and shook his head. "Not at all. The Fourth will be remaining in Sicily to hold the island permanently for Rome. You'll be an administrator, doing nothing more taxing than preparing reports and running inspections. I wouldn't fret about a lost career. Just the opposite. You're on your way up to ranks and duties that require more of a man's head than they do of his arm."

He clapped me on the shoulder:

"Good luck, Centurion!"

On a pleasantly balmy evening a few weeks later, I tried my legs for the first time on the terrace of the villa of Archimedes.

I had asked for this house to be assigned as my residence, and the request had been granted because of my new rank. I had asked to live there not because it was a splendid, comfortable place, but because I wanted to save it from possible desecration by some officer who might not have had any special feeling for the wise, gentle and courageous old man who had once dwelt within its walls.

Cynthia stood beside me on the terrace that evening. Her gown was a pale gray, and her eyes were warm in the fading light. In the harbor below, sailors swarmed over three great galleys that would be making sail and heading for Rome when the sun was up and the tides favorable on the morrow.

"They're carrying Marcellus and his staff back to the Tiber," I said. "In triumph, praise be!"

Cynthia's arm slipped around my waist. The warm touch troubled me a little. I turned, looking at her.

"Are you certain? There'll be precious little money, even though I'm now a centurion."

"I'm certain, my darling." She kissed my mouth. "The barrier of the war is gone. The rest of the barriers—your station, my vanished wealth—they never really mattered. There was never time for me to tell you that, let alone make you understand it."

"Still, people may laugh at you for throwing yourself away on a man like me."

"Being with the man I love most in the world, you mean." She kissed me again. "The subject is closed."

We stood a while, watching the galleys raise their anchors and turn into the scarlet sea. I must have been frowning. She asked what was disturbing me.

I answered, "The memory of my friend, the tribune Terentius. He once told me that for all the blackness in the world, there were moments of light. Moments which make the rest—the fear, the pain—worthwhile. I didn't believe him then. Now I do. There is considerable injustice in the world. Unforgivable. Cruelty, and even madness past believing, sometimes. But now and again, one hour makes it all worth the struggle. Strangest of all—no Roman made me believe that. An enemy did."

And as I stood musing, I recalled a bearded face beneath a cloaked hood in the temple of Artemis.

A skiff had put out from shore, bearing in its bow the commander's standard. Evidently the commander intended to stay aboard the largest galley tonight, in order to be ready for a prompt departure in the morning. As I watched the skiff's progress, something prompted me to say:

"He is a great general. But a greater man."

"Marcellus?"

"Oh yes, that's true, right enough—"

The skiff reached the largest galley.

"But I was thinking of the Carthaginian."

I watched tiny figures board one of the red-lit galleys. The sunset hastened on toward full dark, and the ships riding at anchor were soon blurred into the surrounding shadows of sea and sky. Somewhere in that hour of gentle nightfall, I said a final farewell to one world and turned forever to a new and better one—

A world of love in the eyes of the woman at my side.

# JOHN JAKES

With publication in January, 1976, of the fourth volume of The American Bicentennial Series, John Jakes became the first author in history to have three novels on national best-seller lists within a single year . . . climaxing a twenty-five-year professional writing career which began with sale of a science fiction short story (for $25) to *The Magazine of Fantasy and Science Fiction* in 1951. A native of Chicago and still a Midwestern resident, Jakes sold his first story while in his second year of college, and his first book—an historical Western for young people—twelve months later. Since then he has published more than fifty books and two hundred short pieces ranging from science fiction to suspense, and fiction and nonfiction for young people, including a biography of the Mohawk chief, Joseph Brant, and a history of the TIROS weather satellite program. Most of this work was produced while Jakes held creative posts with advertising agencies, working on behalf of some of America's largest companies; he left advertising in 1970 to write full time. He remains an avid community theater actor and playwright (eleven of his plays and musicals have been published), as well as a lifelong history buff. His interest in history led to half a dozen historical novels— originally written under his "Jay Scotland" pseudonym—which Pinnacle Books is now publishing in completely revised, uniform editions.

Another tumultuous romantic novel
by Patricia Matthews,
author of the multi-million
copy national bestseller,
**LOVE'S AVENGING HEART**

# Love's Wildest Promise

P40-047  $1.95

Sarah Moody was a lady's maid in a wealthy London home. But suddenly her quiet sheltered world was turned upside down when she was abducted and smuggled aboard a ship bound for the colonies. Its cargo—whores to satisfy the appetites of King George's soldiers in New York. Was Sarah destined to become one of these women? Or would she find the man she was searching for, the man who would help her to fulfill Love's Wildest Promise.

If you can't find this book at your local bookstore, simply send the cover price, plus 25¢ for postage and handling to:

 Pinnacle Books
275 Madison Avenue, New York, New York 10016

The epic novel of the Old South,
ablaze with the unbridled passions
of men and women seeking
new heights for their love

# *Windhaven Plantation*

## *Marie de Jourlet*

### P40-022 $1.95

Here is the proud and passionate story of one man—
Lucien Bouchard. The second son of a French nobleman,
a man of vision and of courage, Lucien dares to seek a new
way of life in the New World that suits his own high
ideals. Yet his true romantic nature is at war with his
lusty, carnal desires. The four women in his life reflect
this raging conflict: Edmée, the high-born, amoral
French sophisticate who scorns his love, choosing his
elder brother, heir to the family title; Dimarte, the in-
genuous, earthy, and sensual Indian princess; Amelia,
the fiery free-spoken beauty who is trapped in a life of
servitude for crimes she didn't commit; and Priscilla,
whose proper manner hid the unbridled passion of her
true desires.

"... will satisfy avid fans of the plantation genre."
—*Bestsellers* magazine

If you can't find this book at your local bookstore, simply
send the cover price plus 25¢ for postage and handling to:

 Pinnacle Books
275 Madison Avenue, New York, New York 10016

PN-15

In the tumultuous, romantic tradition of
Rosemary Rogers, Jennifer Wilde, and
Kathleen Woodiwiss

# Love's Avenging Heart

## Patricia Matthews

### P987    $1.95

The stormy saga of Hannah McCambridge, whose fiery
red hair, voluptuous body, and beautiful face made her
irresistible to men...Silas Quint, her brutal stepfather,
sold her as an indentured servant...Amos Stritch, the
lascivious tavernkeeper, bought her and forced her to
submit to his lecherous desires...Malcolm Verner, the
wealthy master of Malvern Plantation, rescued her from
a life of poverty and shame. But for Hannah, her new
life at Malvern was just the beginning. She still had to
find the man of her dreams—the man who could un-
leash the smouldering passions burning inside her and
free her questing heart.

You've read other historical romances, now <u>live</u> one!

---

If you can't find this book at your local bookstore, simply send
the cover price, plus 25¢ for postage and handling to:

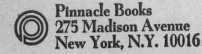

Pinnacle Books
275 Madison Avenue
New York, N.Y. 10016

## "POWERFUL AND EXCITING" —JOHN JAKES
**best-selling author of the American Bicentennial Series**

# The Godson
## by Gloria Vitanza Basile
### P719   $1.95

"THE GODSON is a great big blockbuster. The book deserves success. Not only is the author a compelling writer, but she is thoroughly grounded in the early history of the Mafia. Readable and ringing with authenticity."
> —*Chicago Tribune Book World Review*

"A richly detailed, passionate and panoramic tapestry...a mammoth undertaking, brilliantly conceived and carefully structured."
> —*Bestsellers* magazine

---

If you can't find this book at your local bookstore, simply send the cover price, plus 25¢ for postage and handling to:

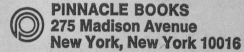

**PINNACLE BOOKS**
**275 Madison Avenue**
**New York, New York 10016**